Jed Cartwright and the
Lost Gold Mine

by Ed Dunlop

PACE Publications, Independence, MO 64055

Jed Cartwright and the Lost Gold Mine
by Ed Dunlop

Cover Illustration by Ron Raymer
Copy Editor: Julia C. Hansen
Proofreaders: Sheri Harshaw and Sally Bradley
Book Design: Amy Haynes

Copyright © 1999
Ed Dunlop
All Rights Reserved

Published by
PACE *Publications*
PO Box 1982
Independence, MO 64055

Printed in the United States of America
Set in Times New Roman 12 point
ISBN 0-918407-14-1

To my daughter, Rebecca

"And he said unto them,
Take heed, and beware of covetousness:
for a man's life consisteth not in the abundance
of the things which he possesseth."
Luke 12:15

Contents

The Stakeout

Jed Cartwright knelt behind a fallen log at the top of the ridge, then cautiously rose up just enough to peer at the wooded glen below. His breath came in short, steamy gasps, and his heart pounded furiously. He was surprised to suddenly realize that he was trembling from the cold air. The sight of the quiet little cabin surrounded by scrubby trees brought back a haunting feeling of fear.

The sheriff spoke in a whisper. "That the place, Boy?"

Jed's gaze darted to the shiny revolver in the man's hand, then back to the silent cabin below. "Yes, sir," he replied. "That's it."

"Yo're sure?"

The boy studied the man's face. "Yes, sir, that's the place, all right."

Jake Cartwright placed a huge hand on Jed's trembling shoulder. "Relax, Son," he said softly. "There's nothing to be afraid of. We have fifteen guns on our side, and there's only two of them."

The boy swallowed hard, then nodded. "I know, Pa," he whispered. "But I get the shakes just thinking about them

two. That night Wolf and I were trapped in the root cellar . . . "
His voice trailed off.

Sheriff Bates spun the cylinder on his revolver, transferred
the weapon to his left hand, and then picked up a fist-sized
rock. "It took courage to come back here, Jed," he said quietly. "The citizens of Missouri appreciate what you did today. Al and Clem Jethers have been robbing stage coaches
and knocking over banks all over the state, and I'm aiming to
put a stop to it! I appreciate you showing us their hideout. We
never would have found it without yore help."

He rose up on one knee and hurled the rock with all his
strength. The missile struck the rough plank door of the little
cabin, and a hollow thud echoed across the hillside. "Al
Jethers!" the lawman shouted. "Clem Jethers! Give yoreselves
up! This is Sheriff Bates! We have the place surrounded! Come
out with yore hands up!"

A thrill of excitement went through Jed. This was an adventure he would remember for the rest of his life! He glanced
over at Pa, who was sighting down the rifle that looked so
small in his huge hands, then across the ravine where the other
men were concealed in the bushes. Suddenly he felt very safe.
"We have 'em, don't we, Pa?" he whispered.

Jed turned and watched the cabin door, but there was no
movement or sign of life. Sheriff Bates hollered again, but as
the echoes of his voice died away, the only response was silence.

The lawman motioned, and two deputies slipped through
the trees and took up positions on either side of the cabin
door, their revolvers drawn and ready. The sheriff slipped
from tree to tree until he was near the door. Gun drawn, he
darted from behind a tree and dashed to the side of the cabin.

When he reached it safely, he slithered along the wall until he was at the door.

The sheriff threw open the cabin door and leaped to one side. Again, he shouted for the bandits to surrender. As before, there was no answer from within the little cabin. The sheriff nodded at the deputies, and the men charged into the building, guns drawn and ready. But the cabin was empty.

The men holstered their weapons and the entire posse crowded in to see the little cabin. "Look at those there cobwebs, Sheriff!" one of the men drawled. "The Jethers ain't been heer fer weeks!"

Jed crowded inside with the men. The cabin was a familiar place to him. He and his dog Wolf had spent several nights there on their way to St. Louis unaware that they were in the hideout of the notorious Jethers brothers, whom he and Wolf had helped put in jail some time earlier.

One of the sheriff's men opened the trap door to the little root cellar, and a thrill of danger swept over Jed as he remembered the night he and Wolf had hidden there when the outlaws had shown up by surprise. The boy and the dog had escaped only after the men had drunk themselves into unconsciousness.

Finally, Sheriff Bates called Pa over to him. "You and Jed might as well head for home," he suggested. "The men and I will stake out the place for a few days, hoping to catch these birds when they come home to roost. But there's no sense in you waiting it out."

He shook Jed's hand. "Thanks, Jed. We'll let you know when we catch those varmints."

Jed smiled. "I wish you could have caught them today," he said.

The sheriff nodded. "So do I, Son, so do I."

He glanced up at Jake Cartwright, who towered over him. "Jake, how about you and the boy takin' the stagecoach back to St. Louis fer us? Looks like we'll be campin' out here fer a spell."

A number of the men went down to the stagecoach with the Cartwrights and unloaded the bedrolls and supplies. "It's gonna be cold vittles for a few days," one of the men grumbled good-naturedly. "Can't have no fires on a stake-out."

The leather seat swayed and bucked as the stage bounced along the rutted road, and Jed pushed his heels hard against the boot rail to keep his seat. It was nearly seven feet to the ground, and the idea of tumbling from the driver's seat of a bouncing coach didn't appeal to him. Pa glanced over and noticed his predicament. "Rough ride, isn't it?" he chuckled.

Jed nodded. "You act like it doesn't even bother you."

Pa shrugged. "I'm used to it. I drove stage for nearly two years when I was younger." He nodded toward the carriage. "Care to ride inside? It's smoother."

The boy shook his head. "I'd rather be up here with you."

They rode in silence for several minutes. Jed studied the huge man as he drove. *Pa's the biggest man I've ever seen,* he told himself, *and probably the kindest. I'm proud he's my Pa!*

He took a deep breath, then asked, "Pa? Are you and Ma sorry you adopted me?"

The big man laughed, and his booming voice startled the horses. He clenched one hand into a huge fist and gently thumped the boy on the knee. "Jed, it's only been a week since you became an official member of our family, but this has been the best week of our lives! We're all very glad that God sent you to us!"

Jed took out his pocketknife and tried to whittle at a stick he had found in the woods. The jerks and bumps made it impossible, and he put them under the seat. Pa drove in silence, then finally spoke again. "Jed, the fever of 1858 claimed a lot of lives," he said, choosing his words carefully, "and I don't understand why God chose to take your Ma and Pa. But He had a purpose in it. And I don't understand why He sent you to live with your Uncle Matt and Aunt Nell, cruel as they were to you."

Jed interrupted. "Those were the worst two years of my whole life!"

Mr. Cartwright nodded thoughtfully. "I know, Jed, I know," he said softly. "But God's hand was on you, even then, and we're grateful that He brought you to St. Louis, and to us."

Later, when they stopped to rest the horses, Jed began again to whittle. Mr. Cartwright glanced at the carving in the boy's hand, and his eyes widened in surprise. "It's a great blue heron, isn't it?"

Jed was pleased. "You can tell already!"

Pa shook his head. "Jed, you amaze me. I can't believe that a twelve-year-old boy can carve like that!"

His adopted son smiled modestly. "Pa taught me. And he was the best!" A thin, white shaving curled away from the wood as the blade of the knife slowly advanced along the length of the stick.

"But I've known men five times your age who have carved all their lives, and they could take lessons from you!" the big man protested. "Jed, you amaze me!"

Jed gripped the carving between his knees, then placed his left hand timidly on Pa's huge shoulder. "Pa?"

The man turned to face him. "Yes, Son?"

"I'm grateful to you and Ma for taking me and Wolf in.

Thank you."

A huge arm went around Jed's shoulder. "You're more than welcome, Son. We're thankful that God sent you to us." The big man glanced at the sky. "We'll be out of daylight soon. I guess we'll spend the night in Festus, then reach Meadow Green sometime tomorrow."

Jed yawned. "It's been a long day. I wish Wolf could have come with us."

 **Accused**

A rabbit leaped from the tall grasses and bounced across the rutted road, and the huge gray dog immediately took off after him. Jed called him back. "Wolf!"

Wolf paused, took one last longing look at the rabbit, then trotted obediently back to his master. "Wolf, you know better than to waste your time on rabbits!" the boy scolded, and the big dog hung his head.

Nathan shook his head in amazement. "I can't believe how well he obeys you!" he exclaimed. "You could see how badly he wanted that rabbit!" He set his lunch bucket in the dust and stroked the huge head with both hands. "I wish I had a dog like him."

His sister Ruth stepped up and scratched Wolf's ears. "Where did you get him, Jed?"

Jed looked from his brother to his sister, pleased at their response to his dog. Nathan was eleven, and his acceptance of Jed had been every bit as enthusiastic as that of his parents. Ruth was eight and had been shy and reserved toward Jed at first. But Jed had won her confidence by making a number of animal carvings for her, and the two had become very close.

Nathan and Ruth had been delighted when Jed was adopted as a member of their family.

"My real Pa gave Wolf to me before he and Ma died," Jed answered, "so he's a very special dog. He's almost like a brother."

Nathan pulled a watch from his pocket, glanced at it, then hurriedly shoved it back in his pocket. "Come on," he urged, "we'd better hurry, or we'll be late for school!"

The three young people resumed their walk with the huge dog trotting alongside Jed. Nathan snickered when he noticed that Jed was carrying Ruth's lunch bucket. "Better not start that," he teased, "or she'll expect you to do it all the time!"

Jed laughed and swung the tin bucket at his brother. "I don't mind," he replied, "as long as I don't have to carry her!"

"Cartwright!" a voice called, "wait for me!" The three turned, and Jed saw a tall, stocky boy with unkempt brown hair hurrying toward them.

"Oh, brother," Ruth muttered, "what does he want?" She turned to Jed. "That's Merle Watkins, our next door neighbor," she explained in a whisper. "He's a bully, and nobody likes him!"

The newcomer was puffing as he caught up with them. "Hey, Cartwright," he taunted Nathan, "I heard that your Pa took in a poor kid!" He glanced at Jed, then pointed a thumb at him as he looked back to Nathan. "Is this him?"

The Cartwrights stood silent, but the tall boy continued. "Hey, poor boy, did you know you're adopted? It's all over town!" He laughed crudely.

Ruth stomped her foot angrily. "Why don't you mind your own beeswax?" she demanded.

Merle ignored her. "You're not a Cartwright!" he sneered at Jed. "You don't even look like one! Look at Ruth and

Nathan! Blond hair, blue eyes. And look at you! Dark hair, and dark eyes! You may live in that big, fancy house, but you're not really a Cartwright. You're just adopted!"

Jed shrugged and looked at Nathan, but Ruth stomped her foot again. "He is too a Cartwright!" she protested. "Why don't you go away and leave us alone!"

The bully grabbed one of Ruth's long braids and twisted it until she cried out in pain. "Why don't you just mind your own beeswax, Miss Smarty?"

Jed dropped the lunch buckets and grabbed Merle by the shirt collar. "Keep your hands off her!" he warned. "If you touch her again, I'll—"

The bigger boy cut him off. "You'll do what, sissy?" he scoffed. "I can clean yore plow any day!" He jerked his shirt out of Jed's grasp.

Nathan stepped up to Jed. "Come on, Jed, don't try to fight him," he pleaded. "He's nothing but trouble! And we've got to get to school!"

"You're afraid, sissy!" the bully taunted. He took a step toward Jed. Wolf chose that moment to make an appearance out of the gooseberry bushes along the side of the road, and the big boy stepped back in surprise and cowardice. "I'll let you go this time," he blustered, watching the huge dog warily, "but next time, it's gonna be a different story!"

The Cartwright kids walked quickly down the road toward school with Wolf still tagging along. "We'll have to really hurry now, or we'll be late for sure," Nathan remarked. The school bell began to ring just as they entered the schoolyard, and they hurried inside with the other pupils. Ruth and Nathan took their seats with the others, and the classroom grew quiet.

Jed stood in the back of the room uncertainly. A bald-headed man sat sternly at a large desk facing the class. As he stood to his feet, Jed saw that he was very tall, and incredibly thin.

He looked in Jed's direction. "Young man," he demanded, "what is your name?"

Jed swallowed hard. "Cartwright, sir," he answered. "Jedediah Cartwright. But my friends call me Jed."

"Very well, Jedediah. I am Mr. Gunderson. Please take the empty seat in the third row for the present. You have missed the first two days of school. I understand that your absence is the fault of our sheriff, Mr. Bates. Your absence will not be held against you—this time. Third grade, take out your spellers."

As Jed took his seat, he felt a sharp, painful kick in the back. He whirled around and was dismayed to find Merle Watkins seated directly behind him! Merle gave him a leering grin, and anger flared in Jed's heart. He glanced at Mr. Gunderson, but the teacher had not seen Merle's actions.

The morning passed quickly. Jed was thrilled to be back in school again. The two years with Uncle Matt and Aunt Nell had been made even more difficult by their refusal to allow him to attend school. The scratch of the chalk on the blackboard, the smell of the ink in the wells, the feel of the pages of the textbooks beneath his fingertips—all were like old, familiar friends, and he thoroughly enjoyed renewing their acquaintances.

At lunchtime the students filed out into the schoolyard with their lunch buckets. The girls found places in the grassy shade of the walnut grove beside the schoolyard, while the boys perched on a fallen oak while they ate. When lunch was finished, the schoolyard echoed with shrieks of laughter as the students played freeze tag. Jed was surprised to notice that Merle refused to take part in the fun.

Finally, the bell rang, and the young people headed for the schoolhouse. Mr. Gunderson met them at the door with a stern look on his thin face. "Take your seats without a single word," he ordered, and the students filed in quietly.

Jed took his seat, then gasped in surprise as he saw the blackboard. A large face had been drawn, with a long nose and tiny, round glasses. The drawing was labeled "Mr. Gunderson." The entire class sat quietly, shocked by the bold defiance of the unknown artist. Mr. Gunderson walked to the front of the room and faced the pupils without saying anything. A full minute went by. The silence was unbearable. Tension filled the little schoolroom, and the younger students squirmed nervously.

Finally, the teacher spoke. "Does anyone," he asked, "have anything they would like to tell me before I deal with this blatant act of impertinence?"

The pupils sat quietly. Mr. Gunderson spoke again. "We'll get to the bottom of this," he said, "if it takes all day! If you know anything about this, you had better speak up now!"

Merle raised his hand. Mr. Gunderson turned toward him. "Yes, Mr. Watkins?"

"I think Jed Cartwright knows something about it," the boy answered. "He came in the schoolhouse by himself while we were playing freeze tag, so he might have drawn that picture. And I saw him put a piece of chalk in his desk just a minute ago."

Jed sat stunned, puzzled by the other boy's accusation. *What is Merle up to?* he wondered. *I don't even know the guy, and he's already trying to get me in trouble!*

Mr. Gunderson walked back to Jed's desk and stood over him. Jed looked up at him anxiously. "What do you know about this, Mr. Cartwright?" the tall man asked sternly.

"Nothing, sir!" Jed stammered. "I didn't do it!"

"Stand up!" the man ordered, and Jed got to his feet and stood beside his desk. The teacher bent down, peering into Jed's desk. "What's this?" he asked, as he withdrew his hand from the compartment of the desk. He held up a stick of chalk, and Jed gasped in surprise.

Mr. Watkins

Jed left the schoolhouse that afternoon with his back burning from the blows of the hickory switch, and with anger burning in his heart toward Merle Watkins. *I'll get even with Merle if it's the last thing I do!* he thought bitterly.

But as he walked home, he remembered how Pa Cartwright had forgiven him for wrecking the expensive surrey that he had stolen back on that first traumatic day in St. Louis. He thought about the fact that the Lord Jesus had forgiven him for his sins, and he knew in his heart that he was to forgive Merle. He prayed as he walked along, "Lord, help me to be able to forgive Merle. And Lord, please help me to stay out of trouble with Mr. Gunderson."

He was almost home when a voice called out, "Hey, Sissy, did you and Mr. Gunderson have a good time this afternoon?" Jed glanced around, but no one was in sight. The voice called again, "Up here, Sissy!" Jed looked up into the branches of a sweet gum hanging over the road, and the leering face of Merle Watkins appeared among the branches. The boy scrambled down and stood in front of Jed.

"Have a good time this afternoon, Sissy?" he asked again.

Jed looked up at the boy. Merle was about two inches taller than he. "You lied about me, Merle," he replied, "and you know it!"

"Oh, did I now!" the taller boy taunted. "Whatcha gonna do about it, huh?"

"I'm not going to do anything about it," Jed answered. "I've decided to just forgive you."

"Well, isn't that sweet!" Merle sneered. "You're gonna forgive me!" His eyes narrowed. "You're yellow, Cartwright! You're afraid to fight!"

"There's no reason to fight," Jed countered. "I'm willing to be friends."

"Be friends?" the boy hooted. "Cartwright, I don't wanna be friends with you! I wanna fight!" He put a hand on Jed's chest and gave him a shove.

Jed decided to ignore the older boy, and tried to step around him. But Merle had no intention of letting Jed pass. He planted one foot behind Jed's and gave Jed a hard shove, knocking him to the ground. As Jed got to his feet, the bigger boy doubled up his fist and swung at him.

Jed saw the punch coming and simply rolled out of the way. That seemed to make the other boy even angrier. He took a step back and said, "All right, Cartwright, you're asking for it!" With that, he came in swinging.

Jed was ready. As Merle swung, Jed nimbly sidestepped and then grabbed the boy's arm. He dropped his stance, swinging his shoulder high at the same time, and neatly flipped the stouter boy over his shoulder. Merle landed heavily in the roadway, momentarily knocking the wind out of him.

Jed started to walk away, but the bully wasn't through. He sprang to his feet and came swinging again. Jed was cautious. The older boy was taller and heavier, and Jed knew he would be at a disadvantage. As Merle's fist lashed out, the younger boy ducked, then landed a punch in the bully's stomach. The boy doubled over in pain. Jed followed through with another punch.

The bully still had not had enough. He shook his head, then came at Jed again, fists flying. One blow caught Jed off guard, and a fist crashed against his jaw, splitting his lip. Jed turned away, then spun around and landed a good punch on Merle's nose.

The boy screamed in pain as his nose began to bleed, and he rushed at Jed again. Jed was ready for him. As Merle lashed out with his right fist, Jed quickly stepped aside, grabbed the boy's arm, and flipped him to the ground just as he had done before. The bully landed on his back, slightly dazed.

Jed sat on the boy's chest. "Merle, I didn't want to fight you, but you made me," he said. "We can be friends, or we can be enemies. It's up to you."

"I'll never be your friend, Cartwright!" the boy muttered through clenched teeth.

"It's your choice," Jed told him as he climbed off and stood to his feet. "But I'd rather be friends with you." He left Merle sitting in the weeds beside the road and walked quickly home.

Jed quietly closed the front door behind him, hoping to slip over to the water basin and wash the blood from his face before anyone saw him. But Wolf was there to meet him with a joyful bark, and he paused to stroke the thick gray fur affectionately. "How ya doing, Wolf?" he crooned. "Have a good day? Mine was a bit rough." He glanced up to see Mrs. Cartwright watching him from the doorway.

Mrs. Cartwright took a step toward him, then stopped short as she saw Jed's bloody lip. "Son," she cried in alarm, "what happened?"

Jed tried to shrug off the injury. "It's nothing, Ma," he protested. "Don't worry about it!"

But the woman turned and called, "Mabel, bring a wet cloth for Jed's face! And hurry!" A heavyset black woman appeared almost instantly with a wet towel, which she handed to her mistress.

Mrs. Cartwright sponged at the cut with the cloth, and Jed winced. "Sorry to hurt you, Son," she said gently, "but we need to clean this up just a bit. Now, what happened?"

Jed told her briefly about the drawing on the chalkboard, and about the fight with Merle Watkins. As he finished, he saw the huge figure of Pa in the kitchen doorway. Mr. Cartwright was a giant of a man, standing nearly seven feet tall, with arms and shoulders that told of his tremendous strength.

"Pa," Jed said, "I wasn't going to fight him. I tried not to!"

Pa nodded sympathetically. "You did the right thing, Son," he said. "Never fight unless you have to. But to tell the truth, I'm glad you won! Merle Watkins has quite a reputation as a bully, but none of the other kids can stand up to him. Do your best to stay out of his way, but remember to pray for him also. He and his family need the Lord."

"Oh dear," Ma worried aloud, "I hope this won't lead to more trouble with that hateful family!"

Pa turned to her. "Deborah," he said gently but firmly, "let's leave it in the hands of the Lord, shall we?"

The next afternoon, Jed walked home from school with Ruth and Nathan. "Jed, do you think Merle will try to fight you again?" Ruth asked, biting her lip as she looked up into his face. "He told Arlis Adams today that he was going to beat you up!"

Jed pulled one of her blond braids playfully as he replied, "I hope not, little sis! I'll try not to fight him again, unless I have to."

Nathan tugged at his arm. "Jed! Look!"

Pa was just driving a new surrey into the driveway. The young people ran over to see it. The surrey was blue and gold, with a red and white top trimmed in gold fringe. Jed realized that it was identical to the one he had wrecked the day he first met Pa.

Pa hopped down from the carriage. "Hi, gang!" he greeted them. He turned to Jed and Nathan. "Boys, I got something in the back that I think you'll like!" He reached behind the seat and lifted out two long flat boxes, then handed one to each boy. The boxes were heavy. The boys forgot all about the new surrey.

"What's in these?" Jed wanted to know.

Pa just laughed that booming laugh of his. "Why don't you open them and find out?" he chuckled. His eyes were twinkling.

The boys tore into the boxes. Jed had his opened first, and pulled out a shiny new rifle! "This is super!" he said, laughing in delight. "What kind of a rifle is this?"

The new rifle was much shorter than Pa's ancient rifle "Old Betsy" had been. It had no percussion lock, and there was a strange handle mechanism behind the trigger. The polished walnut stock was satin smooth. Jed glanced at Nathan's rifle. It was identical to his.

Jed looked up at Pa. "Thanks, Pa!" he grinned. "This is super! But I've never seen guns like these before! 'Old Betsy' didn't look like this!"

Pa Cartwright grinned broadly. "These are new-fangled

Spencer repeating rifles!" he said proudly. "They can fire seven shots without reloading! The lever behind the trigger chambers a new shell each time you pull it down."

Jed was amazed. "Seven shots?" he echoed. He looked at the rifle again. "Where do you put the percussion caps?"

Pa laughed. "These rifles don't use percussion caps," he explained, "or even black powder, for that matter. All you do to load is insert a shell through this little port in the receiver. You can put in seven bullets, and fire seven times without reloading! Each time you cock the lever, it throws out the shell that was fired and puts a new one in."

Jed was amazed. He looked at Nathan. "Isn't this keen?" he exclaimed. "You and I can go hunting together!"

Pa handed Jed a small box. "These are the shells," he said. "We can go and try out the new guns right now, if you like."

Nathan handed his lunch bucket to Ruth, and she took it into the house. The boys scrambled after their father into the new surrey, and the three of them went to park the carriage in the carriage house. They carried the new rifles out behind the barn, and Jed watched in amazement as Pa loaded one. The man slipped seven shiny brass cartridges into the gun, and then handed the weapon to Jed.

"See that corn cob sitting on that fence post?" he asked. "See if you can knock it off!"

Jed found the cob in the sights of the new gun and pulled the trigger. Nothing happened. Pa laughed. "You didn't cock the rifle, Jed!" he chuckled. "Pull the lever all the way down, then all the way back up." Jed followed his instructions, aimed again, and pulled the trigger. There was a loud report from the rifle, and the cob flew from the fence post.

Pa was impressed. He took the rifle from Jed, then walked over to the post. "Nice shot, Son!" he commented as he set the corncob back on the post.

He returned to where the boys stood and handed the rifle to Nathan. "Give it a try, Nathan." The boy took the gun awkwardly. Jed could tell he was a little afraid of it. But he cocked the weapon, sighted down the barrel, and squeezed the trigger.

"Not bad, Son!" Mr. Cartwright encouraged. "Try it again!" On the fifth shot, Nathan hit the cob.

When the seventh shot was fired, Mr. Cartwright picked up the other rifle and loaded it. The boys practiced shooting until the whole box of ammunition was gone. "I've only got two more boxes, boys," Mr. Cartwright said. "We'd better save them for some real hunting."

The boys sighed, but nodded in agreement. Grinning happily, they carried the new repeating rifles back to the mansion. Jed was so excited about the new rifle that he had forgotten all about checking out the new surrey.

As the trio stepped up on the veranda, Pa turned to Jed. "I saw Sheriff Bates in town today," he said. "The posse waited several days at the Jethers brothers' hideout, but no one ever showed. The posse finally had to leave."

"Then the Jethers are still at large," Jed said.

Mr. Cartwright sighed. "I'm afraid so."

The next Saturday, Jed and Nathan went squirrel hunting in the woods behind the cornfield. Wolf trotted along beside the boys. "Hunting is a lot of fun!" Jed told Nathan. "I'll show you how!" They tramped through the woods a short distance until they came to a split rail fence.

"This is the edge of our property," Nathan told Jed. "But I don't think Mr. Watkins will mind us hunting on his land."

The boys and the dog crossed the fence, and a short while later Jed saw a squirrel's nest overhead in a tall oak. "This is it!" he told his brother. "Now to see if the occupants are home!" Just then, a large gray squirrel scampered across a thick branch and darted around behind the trunk of the tree. Jed pointed him out to Nathan. "Stay here!" he told Nathan. "I'll walk around the other side of the tree, and the squirrel will come around on this side to get away from me. When he does, you get him!"

Nathan nodded, and cocked the rifle nervously. Jed circled the tree, and a moment later, Nathan fired. "I missed him!" he hissed to Jed. Jed just held a finger to his lips and pointed upwards. Nathan looked up, spotted the squirrel again, and fired three more shots, but still no squirrel. He shook his head in disgust. "I'll never learn how to do this!" he said.

Jed walked over to him. "Sure you will!" he encouraged. "It just takes a little practice. We didn't get much target practice in on Monday."

The boys walked deeper into the woods but didn't see any more of the furry little rodents. The leaves were just beginning to change, and Jed admired the beauty of the fall colors. "Fall is coming early this year," he observed. Nathan nodded, still disappointed that he had missed the shot at the squirrel.

In the distance, a bell began to ring, and Nathan turned to Jed. "We'd better head back," he told his brother. "Mabel has dinner ready!"

Jed nodded. "I'm starved!" he said. "Let's hurry!"

As they shuffled back through the woods, a thin man leaped from behind a tree and confronted the boys. He held an old shotgun in his hands, which he pointed at them. "Hold it right there!" he snarled angrily. "What are you doin' on my land?"

Jed quickly grabbed Wolf by the collar. The man pointed

the shotgun at him. "No more sudden moves, Sonny, or I'll blast ya!"

"Mr. Watkins!" Nathan said. "You know me! I'm Nathan Cartwright! This is my brother Jed. We were just squirrel hunting!"

The angry man didn't relax. "Cartwright!" he spat out. "I thought so! Ya boys hear me, and hear me well! The next time I catch a Cartwright on my property, I'll shoot! Do ya hear me?"

"Yes, sir!" the boys answered nervously. The shotgun was still pointed in their direction.

The man eyed Wolf. "Boy," he told Jed, "I better not catch that mangy mutt on my land neither, or I'll put a bullet through his heart! You hear me?" Without waiting for an answer, he suddenly motioned toward the Cartwright estate with the muzzle of the shotgun. "Now git!" he ordered. "And don't let me catch you over here again!"

Jed and Nathan hurried through the woods, glancing nervously over their shoulders from time to time. Mr. Watkins kept the shotgun pointed in their direction until they were out of sight. Still trembling, the boys were only too happy to scramble over the split rail fence and arrive safely on Cartwright property. Nathan let out his breath in a long sigh of relief. "That was Mr. Watkins," he told Jed. "He's Merle's Pa."

Jed nodded. "It's easy to see where Merle gets his meanness!"

The boys hurried to the house, put the guns away, and then washed up quickly for dinner. The family was just bowing for prayer as Jed and Nathan slid into their seats. Mr. Cartwright looked up disapprovingly.

After prayer, Nathan told Pa about the encounter with the

angry neighbor. Mr. Cartwright frowned as he heard the story. "I've been afraid of something like this," he said finally. "That man is the most obstinate man I've ever met! And I do believe that he would carry out his threats!"

He looked from one boy to another. "Both of you stay clear of his property, understand?" The boys nodded. "And you'll have to do your best to keep Wolf off his land, too."

Pa glanced at Ma and recognized the fear that was written in her eyes. He laid a huge, gentle hand on hers. "Don't worry," he tried to reassure her. "Everything's going to be all right. But this is one of those times when it is difficult to respond as a Christian ought."

But that was not the end of the trouble. On Sunday afternoon, Jed took his little sister Sarah for a walk. As he bent over to put her in the baby buggy, she reached up and grabbed two handfuls of his hair, twisting them tightly in her chubby little fists. He winced, and carefully disentangled her fingers from his hair. She giggled happily as he tousled her golden curls.

Jed pushed the buggy carefully across the bumpy fields toward the creek. When they reached the creekbank, he stared in astonishment. The creek was gone.

More Trouble

Jed stood on the bank of the creek, staring in astonishment. The creek was no longer flowing. Yesterday, the water had been nearly three feet deep in places, and now, there was just a sandy channel, with an occasional small pool of murky water. Dozens of fish and hundreds of minnows were trapped in the shallow pools.

The boy left his sister in the baby buggy and ran down to the edge of one of the pools. He couldn't believe his eyes. What could have happened? A creek couldn't just dry up in one day!

Puzzled, Jed pushed the buggy back across the fields. Sarah laughed as the buggy bounced and bumped over the rough ground, but Jed didn't even notice. When they reached the mansion, Jed parked the buggy on the porch behind the house and lifted Sarah out. As he walked into the house, he saw Nathan and handed Sarah to him.

"She's wet!" he laughed as Nathan took his little sister. "You change her! I did it last time!"

He hurried through the house and found his father in the library. "Come out to the creek with me, Pa!" he urged. "Something really strange has happened!"

Moments later, the boy and the huge man stood on the creekbank, staring at the dying creek. Pa frowned. "This isn't natural, Jed," he said. "We need to find out what's causing this!" He glanced up the sandy channel of the creekbed. "Let's go upstream a ways," he suggested, "and see if we can find the cause of the problem. I can't imagine what would make this happen!"

Jed followed his Pa as he walked upstream along the creekbank. In a few minutes, they came to a newly built section of split rail fence. The wood of the fence was still white and fresh, and the fence stretched right across the empty creekbed! Pa frowned when he saw it. "I don't like the looks of this," he muttered.

The two Cartwrights climbed over the fence and continued to follow the path of the creek. Several hundred yards from the new fence, they came to an earthen dam built right across the channel of the creekbed! A new channel had been dug right beside the dam, and the water now flowed down a gully and away from the original creekbed!

Pa angrily hurled his hat to the ground. "If that doesn't beat all!" he fumed. "Someone has diverted the creek so it no longer flows across our property! I'd guess that it rejoins the original course down below the Ledbetters' farm."

He looked at Jed. "Do you know what this means?" he asked. "We'll have to haul water from the well for our livestock! What a job that will be each day! And, it could deplete our well."

A branch snapped, and Jed and his Pa looked up to see Mr. Watkins step from behind a tree. The familiar shotgun was in his hands. "Cartwright!" he called. "What are you doin' nosin' around on my property?"

Pa looked up the slope at the man. "Mr. Watkins, is this your doing?" he asked. "This creek has been diverted, so it no longer waters our property!"

The neighbor laughed. "I guess I can take credit for it!" he boasted. "My men and I have been working on this little project for three days!"

"But Meadow Green needs the creek!" Pa protested. "We'll have to haul water for our livestock if the creek is no longer running."

Mr. Watkins just grinned. "Sorry, neighbor," he laughed, "but I guess that's yore problem, not mine." His eyes narrowed, and he gestured with the weapon in his hands. "Now," he hissed, "you and your boy git yoreselves off my land! And don't let me catch you over here again, or I'll fill you with buckshot!"

Pa picked up his hat and tried to reason with Mr. Watkins. But the man just laughed at him. "Save yore breath, Cartwright," he said, "nothin's gonna change! And you and the boy had better git movin' afore I lose my patience with ya!"

The Cartwrights hurried back to Meadow Green. Back at the mansion, Pa called the servants together and explained the situation to them. "We're not going to do anything to retaliate," he said firmly. "We'll just have to haul water for the stock for a few days until I have the chance to reason with the man."

"I know how to reason with him," one of the field hands muttered. "Just give me a loaded revolver!"

Pa shook his big head. "That's just the kind of thing we want to avoid!" he said. "Watkins is hoping for a fight, but he's not going to get one from us! Do I make myself clear?"

But the trouble with the neighbor continued. Monday

morning as the young people were preparing for school, there was a knock at the front door. Silas opened it to find Mr. Watkins standing there. With him was Sheriff Bates. Silas called Mr. Cartwright to the door, and Jed joined them with a growing sense of dread.

The sheriff looked at Pa apologetically. "Sorry to trouble you, Jake, but this man has a complaint against you," he said. He turned to the neighbor. "Tell Jake what you told me."

Mr. Watkins stepped forward eagerly. "Cartwright," he snarled, "yore boy's dog has been killing my sheep! I lost two lambs and a ewe last night! I want the dog shot!"

Jed stared at the man in horror. "Wolf didn't do it!" he protested. "He wouldn't kill sheep!"

"I've got proof!" the neighbor insisted. "Yore dog's tracks are all over the place! And I've got three dead sheep." He turned to the sheriff. "I want the dog killed!" he announced.

Sheriff Bates turned to Pa. "I'm sorry," he said, "but if what he says is true, we'll have to destroy the dog!"

"Let's not be too hasty!" Mr. Cartwright interjected. He turned to Jed. "Was Wolf in the house all night?"

Jed nodded. "Yes, sir. He slept in my room. And he never left until I let him out this morning!"

Mr. Cartwright looked sternly at Mr. Watkins. "I'm sorry that you lost sheep," he said, "but it wasn't Jed's dog that did it! Perhaps it was a pack of strays."

The neighbor shook his head vehemently. "No such thing, Cartwright! Come look at the tracks! There's not another dog in the county that could leave tracks as big as these!" He turned to the sheriff again. "I want the dog killed!" he insisted.

Pa turned to Jed again. "Get ready for school, Son." He laid a huge, gentle hand on the boy's shoulder. "I'll handle this."

"But, Pa!" Jed protested. "He wants to kill Wolf!"

The big man nodded. "We both know Wolf is innocent," he agreed. "Nobody's going to shoot him unless there's a mighty big heap of hard evidence!"

Mr. Watkins grinned in anticipation. "I've got the evidence!" he crowed. "Just wait and see! The dog is guilty, and I've got the proof!"

Westward Bound

Jed squirmed and fidgeted in his seat. He couldn't keep his mind on his studies. *Mr. Watkins wants to kill Wolf!* A sudden, worrisome thought entered Jed's troubled mind. *What if Wolf is guilty? Could he somehow have gotten out last night? What if Pa and I can't prove that Wolf is innocent?* The thought of life without his big friendly dog made Jed feel sick and empty inside.

Finally, Mr. Gunderson dismissed school, and Jed was the first one out the door. He ran all the way home. His breath was coming in gasps when he reached Meadow Green. Jed stopped at the edge of the driveway. Wolf was not there to meet him. In horror, Jed realized what that meant. No! It couldn't be! They couldn't have shot his dog!

Jed dashed up the driveway. His heart pounding madly, the horrified boy threw open the front door. To his immense relief, a huge gray dog nearly knocked him over as he stepped inside. Jed dropped his jacket and grabbed Wolf, hugging him tightly.

Pa came into the foyer and chuckled as he saw the boy on his knees. "Take it easy, Son!" he laughed. "You'll choke that poor animal to death!"

Jed jumped to his feet. "What happened, Pa?" he asked eagerly. "When Wolf didn't come out to meet me, I was afraid . . ." His voice trailed off.

Pa nodded. "We'll have to keep him in the house for a while," he said. "The way Mr. Watkins is acting right now, we can't take a chance on him or one of his men getting a shot at Wolf."

"But what happened today?" Jed begged again. "Did you see the evidence that Mr. Watkins said he had?"

The big man nodded again. "Sheriff Bates and I went over with Mr. Watkins to the site where the sheep were killed last night. He was right—there were plenty of tracks! But, they weren't made by Wolf! Watkins insisted that they were, until I had Wolf walk through the mud right beside the other tracks. Wolf's tracks were bigger. I think the other tracks were made by a gray wolf."

Jed's eyes grew wide. "You mean that Wolf's tracks are bigger than a real wolf's?" he asked.

Pa laughed happily. "At least we know that Wolf isn't guilty," he said. "Sheriff Bates was convinced, too. He warned Mr. Watkins about causing any more trouble for Wolf."

That evening, as the Cartwright family was gathered for Bible reading and prayer, Pa made a startling announcement. "I'm going to be gone for a while," he said. "I'll be going out west on business, out to Hard Luck near Pike's Peak. I hate to leave while all this trouble with Mr. Watkins is going on, but I have no choice. The railroads want me to meet with some cattle ranchers about purchasing right-of-ways."

Mrs. Cartwright smiled at him. "How long will you be gone, dear?"

Pa frowned. "That's the bad part," he said. "By the time I

make the trip out there, take care of business, and make the trip back, it will be about two months."

"Take us with you!" Nathan suggested. "Then you won't have a chance to get lonely."

Pa shook his head. "I'd like to," he said, "but I'm afraid it would be a rather hard trip for Ma and Sarah. It's almost nine hundred miles each way! And besides, you have school."

"Why don't you just take Nathan and me?" Jed suggested. "We could stand the trip! And we wouldn't miss school that much."

Pa laughed. "Nice try, Son. But I'm afraid not. I'd love to have your company, but your schooling comes first."

Mrs. Cartwright spoke up. "Why not take the boys? You could hire a tutor for the trip, and they would be current with their schooling when they get back."

The big man scratched his jaw thoughtfully. "Never thought of that," he said. "You just might have an idea there!"

Jed and Nathan glanced at each other, then held their breath while Pa considered the idea. "I'll tell you what I'm going to do," he said finally. "I'm going to postpone my trip until Monday. That'll give me a couple of days to try to find a tutor that is willing to go on a trip like this. If I find the right tutor, we'll hire a stagecoach and an extra team of fresh horses, and you both can go. Fair enough?"

"Yippee!" Nathan cheered. "What do you think of that, Jed?"

The next afternoon, Pa rode into the driveway just as Jed and Ruth were leaving to take Wolf for a walk. "It's all set, Son!" Pa called out to the boy. "We leave Monday morning! I found a young teacher by the name of Mr. Phelps. You'll like him."

Jed grinned, excited about the prospect of the trip.

"Thanks, Pa!" he said. "I'll run in and tell Nathan!"

Pa shook his head. "No, sir," he said, "I want to have the fun of telling him myself!"

Wolf barked, and Jed turned back to Pa. "Can Wolf go, too?" he asked eagerly.

Pa thought for a moment. "Maybe that would be best," he agreed. "Then we'll know for sure that he won't trespass on Mr. Watkins' property while we're gone."

The Cartwrights packed for the trip Sunday evening after they returned from church. The boys made certain that their new rifles were included. "Better head for bed, gents," Pa suggested when they had finished packing and all the luggage was stacked in the foyer. "Five o'clock is going to come mighty early."

Early the next morning the Cartwrights and the tutor, Mr. Phelps, met outside the stagecoach depot. Mr. Phelps was a thin man with a shock of unruly black hair and thick spectacles. He spoke in a high-pitched voice with a nasal twang, but he was friendly, and the boys liked him immediately.

"Glad to make your acquaintance, boys," he replied when the introductions were made. "We'll wait an hour or two for the sun to come up, then we'll get started on your lessons."

Pa laughed and laid a hand on Mr. Phelps' shoulder. "Let the boys enjoy the trip today," he told him. "There will be plenty of time for school work tomorrow."

In a few minutes, their goodbyes had been said, and they jolted away from the depot, the Cartwright party the only ones on board the coach. Ruth and Mrs. Cartwright waved from the platform, Ruth crying and Ma close to tears.

The rhythm of the coach wheels made Jed drowsy, and he settled deeper into the plush satin cushions of the seat. He drifted off, lulled to sleep by the music of the rapidly spinning wheels.

When he awoke, the sun was up. He sat up groggily and looked out the window. The stage was passing through a wooded area, and tree branches flashed by the window. "How far have we come?" he asked.

"We've just begun," Pa laughed. "Relax and enjoy the trip. We've still got many miles to go!"

The miles flew by. Jed told Nathan of some of the adventures he and Wolf had experienced during the long walk to St. Louis. "This is really the way to travel," Jed finished. "This beats walking, any day!"

The boy turned to Mr. Cartwright. "There's something I've been wondering since I came to live with you," he said. "Why are we so rich? How did we get all our money?"

The big man laughed. Jed noticed that Mr. Phelps leaned forward, waiting for the answer. Wolf had been sleeping on the floor of the coach, and he sat up and yawned at just that moment, revealing his huge fangs. Mr. Phelps jumped back, startled, and dropped his glasses on the coach seat. The boys could hardly hold back the snickers.

"Jed," Pa began, "just after your Ma and I were married, quite a while before Nathan was born, we headed west so I could be a partner in a silver mining operation with my brother, Andrew. The first couple of years, the mine paid off handsomely, and we made quite a little money. After two or three years, I got tired of the whole thing, and sold out. I invested most of our profits in cattle, railroad stock, and other ventures. It sometimes seems that God has blessed everything I have ever touched.

"My brother, however, stayed with the mining. Shortly after I left, the ore vein played out, and the mine has not produced anything since. Andrew has invested in several other mines, but none of them have produced anything at all. To-day, he is nearly broke, and sad to say, is very bitter against God."

He looked at Jed. "So I guess that's the story of the Cartwright money." He looked thoughtful. "One thing I have learned, boys, is this—money doesn't make anybody happy! I've lived with money, and I've lived without it. Either way, it doesn't produce happiness. But I have seen money produce a lot of greed and misery!"

About noon, they came to a stagecoach stop where they switched horses. Wolf sprang from the coach the minute the door was opened, and Jed ran with him through the little town. For lunch a widow named Rosa served them rabbit stew with potatoes, carrots, and onions. Everyone had a hunk of corn bread, but Jed shared his with Wolf.

The afternoon wore on as the miles rolled by. Every few hours they stopped to rest and water the horses. Shortly after sunset, the stage slowed and Jed looked out the window. They were in another little town. The driver stopped in front of a small, friendly-looking inn.

"We've made good time today, sir," the driver told Mr. Cartwright as he opened the door for his passengers. "We've done nearly sixty miles today."

Well done," Pa answered as he climbed from the coach and stretched his cramped legs.

Pa flipped the man a silver dollar, and he caught the coin in the air. "Thank you, sir! I'll see to your luggage."

Mr. Cartwright went into the inn and reserved a room for himself, the boys, and Mr. Phelps. After a dinner of roast beef and English pudding, the weary travelers retired to their rooms.

The next day, they hit the road again very early. Mr. Phelps began academic exercises with his students as the coach rolled along. The coach bumped and swayed, and Jed and Nathan found it hard to write on their slates, but neither boy complained. They were thankful to be included on the trip.

An hour or so before noon, the coach suddenly swayed as the driver drew back on the reins to stop the horses. He leaned down and called Mr. Cartwright's name. Pa stuck his head out the window. "What is it?" he asked.

"Some sort of trouble ahead, sir," the man responded. He drew a revolver from under the seat, checked it, and then laid it on the seat beside him. Mr. Phelps leaned forward with a worried frown creasing his thin features.

 **Outlaws**

Pa looked up at Mr. Atkins, frowning as he asked, "What kind of trouble?" He craned his neck forward, trying to see the road ahead.

"It looks like a wagon is stopped in the road," the driver answered. "Shall we stop?"

"By all means!" Mr. Cartwright answered. "We may be able to help."

Moments later, the coach drew alongside a heavily loaded wagon. Jed and Nathan stuck their heads out the window. A tired-looking man was standing at the side of the road, hat in hand, staring at the body of a mule lying in the roadway. A look of desperation was on the man's face. As the travelers watched, the man pulled on the harness of the mule, trying to lift the animal's head. "Git up, Jenny!" the man pleaded. "You've gotta git up!"

Jed looked at the wagon. Household goods and a few items of worn furniture were stacked high, and a thin woman and four dirty children in tattered clothing sat forlornly on the seat of the buckboard wagon. Tear-streaked faces turned toward him as he watched.

It was immediately apparent what had happened. The family was moving west, and their tired mule had died on the way. The family was stranded.

"Can we help you, neighbor?" Pa asked, as he approached the man.

The man looked up at Pa, a hopeless look of despair on his face. He ran a dirty hand across his mouth before he spoke. "I don't think so, friend," he answered slowly. "I'm afraid we've just about reached the end of the road. I don't think there is much help for us."

Pa laid a huge hand on the man's shoulder. "Tell me about your problem," he said softly.

The man hung his head as he replied, "We're at the end of the road, mister, that's the problem! Ma and I and the young'uns are trying to move to Oregon. My brother has work for me there. Three days ago, one of my mules died. And now, Jenny here is giving it up." He looked at Pa. "It's a long ways to Oregon, mister, when ya ain't got no mules!"

Pa smiled at the man. "I understand," he said gently. The man looked at the stagecoach, then at Pa's fine tailor-made clothes. "I don't think you do, mister," he replied in a flat voice.

"I've been where you are, neighbor," Pa replied, "more than once!" Pa smiled at the man, then suggested, "Sir, we passed through a town just a few miles back. I'm a fairly good judge of horseflesh. Suppose we take you back to town and buy you a new team?"

The man shook his head and answered bitterly, "It ain't quite that easy, mister! We ain't got no money!" Jed recognized the despair in the man's voice, and his heart went out to him.

"Neighbor," Pa said gently, "perhaps the Lord sent us

along today just to encourage you. I'm talking about buying a new team for you."

The man shook his head, still not understanding what Pa was saying. "I told you, sir, we ain't got no money!"

Pa tried again. "Neighbor, I'm talking about buying the team with my money. I'd like to give you a pair of horses as a gift."

The man's head snapped up as the meaning of Pa's offer sank in. Then, his eyes narrowed, and he looked at Pa suspiciously. "What are you wantin' from us?" he asked.

Pa smiled. "Just a chance to help a fellow traveler," he replied. He held out his hand, and the man slowly took it. "I'm Jake Cartwright," Pa said, "and my sons and I are traveling to Pike's Peak. We saw your wagon, and thought we'd just stop to help."

The man nodded at the introduction. "I'm Dan Spriggs," he mumbled, "and that's my wife and young'uns."

Mr. Cartwright called to the occupants of the coach. "Boys! Mr. Phelps! Come out here a minute!" Nathan flung the door open, and the three scrambled out. "Mr. Phelps," Pa said, "why don't you and the boys stay here with Mrs. Spriggs and the children? Mr. Spriggs and I will head back into town with Mr. Atkins and see if we can find some horses to buy."

The men rode off, and Jed approached the wagon. Five pairs of eyes watched him timidly. Jed saw a little girl, no more than three years old peeking at him from behind her mother's faded dress. "Hi, sweetheart!" he called to the little tike, "would you like to pet my doggie?" To his surprise, the little one stepped out from behind her mother, nodded, and held out her thin little arms to him. Jed lifted her down from the wagon and whistled for Wolf. In no time at all, the four children were all over the dog and the boy, laughing and chattering excitedly.

The woman smiled at Jed. *She looks younger and prettier,* Jed thought, *when she smiles.* The hours went by, and the boys and the dog amused the children while Mr. Phelps sat under a tree and talked to Mrs. Spriggs.

Finally, a dust cloud wound its way down the road toward them, and the stage came into view. Trotting smartly at the rear of the coach were a pair of beautifully matched black mares. Jed ran forward and admired them as the door of the coach opened. "They're beauties, Pa!" he called.

Mr. Cartwright laughed. "We paid a hundred dollars for the pair," he said, "but I'm sure they're worth every penny! Nicest pair of three-year-olds I laid eyes on in a long time. The Oregon trip should be a breeze for these two."

He turned to Mr. Spriggs. "Come on, Dan," he urged, "let's get 'em hitched up, and get you on your way. You've lost enough time already."

The man hesitated. "I still don't understand why you are doing this," he said slowly, almost fearfully. "You don't even know us!"

Pa smiled. "Dan," he said, "everything I have belongs to God. He told me to stop and help you, and I simply obeyed. I wanted to give you these horses in the name of the Lord Jesus."

The man looked sober as he replied, "I've met Christians afore, but they wasn't real. I've never met a real Christian."

Pa smiled sadly. "I hope you have now, Dan."

The man nodded. "Maybe you've got something there."

"Dan," Pa continued, "the greatest gift of all is eternal life through Jesus Christ. He died for your sins, and He offers you salvation as a free gift!"

The other man shook his head. "I ain't ready for that," he replied, "but you've given me something to think about."

As they led the mares to the wagon, the children came running, eager to see the new horses. They gathered around the two mares, chattering excitedly. Mr. and Mrs. Spriggs hugged each other with tears streaming down their faces.

The men helped Mr. Spriggs hitch up the two horses, and then said their good-byes. Mr. Spriggs approached Pa. "Thank you again, sir," he said. "We'll remember you for the rest of our lives!"

Pa shook the hand that was offered. "I was glad to do it, Dan," he said. He placed three ten-dollar gold pieces in the man's hand. "I'd like you to take this," he said. "It will get some food for those young'uns, and some feed for those new horses as you travel to Oregon."

Mr. Spriggs looked at the coins in his hand, then shook his head. "I couldn't," he said, "You've already done more than enough."

But the big man insisted. "Go on, take it!" he replied. "I believe that God wants you to have it."

The man pocketed the money. "God bless you, sir! You're a big man," he said, "but your heart's even bigger! I don't know how we can ever repay you!"

Pa waved as he headed for the coach. "Take care of those young'uns," he called, "and have a safe trip to Oregon!"

As the stagecoach pulled away, Jed poked his head out the window and looked back at the wagon. The horses were trotting merrily along, the man was smiling, the woman was crying, and the children were singing.

"Well, so much for the miles today," Pa laughed. "We'll have to be sure to get an early start tomorrow."

Jed rode in silence for a while, deep in thought. Finally he spoke. "Pa, remember what you said yesterday?"

Pa turned to him. "About what, Jed?"

"About money not making anybody happy," he answered. "It sure seems that money made that family happy today!"

Mr. Cartwright shook his head. "No, Jed," he answered, "money did not make the Spriggs family happy! They were happy because a need was met and they were able to continue their journey. But, it was not money that made them happy. Do you know who enjoyed the gift of the horses most of all today?"

Jed looked up at him. "Who?"

Pa chuckled. "Me! I had more fun than anybody did today, because I was the one who got to do the giving! Jesus told us that it is more blessed to give than to receive, and I experienced that today! Happiness comes from living for Christ and helping others, never from money or the things it will buy."

The sun was setting as Pa called out to Mr. Atkins, "Hey Phillip! Let's do a few more miles, and then just find a place to camp tonight! We can do some heavy miles tomorrow!"

Night was falling quickly and darkness descended upon the weary travelers. Mr. Atkins finally pulled the stagecoach into a little grove of trees. "We can camp here for the night," he said. While he chocked the wheels of the stagecoach and tethered the horses, the others gathered firewood and soon had a roaring fire going. Bedrolls were spread upon the ground. After a meal of beans and cornbread, the travelers retired for the night.

For the next few days, the party traveled on stopping only to rest the horses and sleep at stagecoach way stations along the way. They stopped on Sunday for a day of rest and sang hymns together and read a long passage from the Bible. Then for several days, the party traveled on stopping only to rest the horses and to sleep at night. Occasionally they saw other traveler's heading to Pike's Peak, and sometimes they saw familiar faces at the stagecoach inns.

As the next week of travel drew to a close, the boys caught their breath when the morning light faintly outlined the mighty Rocky Mountains. Pa and the driver both were wearing revolvers on their hips. "This is a rugged area," Pa had explained to Jed and Nathan.

Late in the afternoon, Pa announced, "We should be able to see Pike's Peak in the morning. Tomorrow, if all goes well, we'll reach Hard Luck before dark!" The others cheered. It had been a good trip, but they were all tired of the constant swaying and jolting of the coach.

The road became more rugged, and the horses were tired. After topping a small rise, the driver brought the coach to a stop. "There's a fallen tree in the road!" he called to Mr. Cartwright as he scrambled down from his seat. Pa left the coach, and the two men strained together to move the heavy tree.

"Let's go help them!" Jed called to Nathan. He reached for the handle of the coach door, then froze as he heard a shout. Two men sprang from behind a large boulder at the side of the road. Handkerchiefs covered their faces and they both held revolvers. Their guns trained on Pa and the driver, the bandits shouted, "Hands over your heads! One false move, and you're dead!"

Quietly they raised their hands. Inside the coach, Mr. Phelps covered his face with his hands. "We're being robbed!" he moaned.

Pike's Peak

Jed reached beneath the coach seat and pulled out his rifle. He found the box of shiny brass shells and quickly loaded four into the gun. With trembling hands, he pulled down the lever and cocked the rifle. Quietly, he opened the coach door. Placing one foot out on the coach step, Jed leveled the rifle and took careful aim. His sights trained on the gun hand of one of the robbers, Jed took a deep breath and squeezed the trigger.

The rifle barked, and the robber's gun flew from his hand. He clutched his wrist in pain. The other robber spun around and pointed his revolver at Jed. But Pa had seen Jed slip out the door of the coach, and he was ready. The instant Jed shot, Pa had his own revolver out of its holster. He leaped forward and struck the gun from the bandit's hand.

Pointing his gun at the man's heart, Pa boomed, "Get your hands up, both of you!" Both men raised their hands over their heads. The injured man still clutched his bleeding right hand with his left.

The driver produced a length of rope, and he and Pa quickly tied up the pair of bandits. "Into the coach," Pa ordered, as he pulled the masks from the faces of the men. "We'll give you a free ride into town!"

Pa turned the men over to a deputy sheriff while Mr. Phelps found rooms for the night. Jed was still shaking as he tried to go to sleep that night.

The next morning, Pa was up before daybreak. "Let's move!" he called as he roused the others.

That evening, the stagecoach followed a winding trail that snaked through tall, rocky mountains. Jed stared out the coach window in fascination. The mountains were bare except for occasional trees and bushes and were divided by deep canyons and gorges. "This sure doesn't look like the mountains in Kentucky!" he remarked.

The stage began making its way slowly down into a steep canyon. A cluster of weather-beaten buildings snuggled against the foot of the mountain. "Hard Luck!" the new driver called from his seat atop the coach, and his passengers cheered.

The boys peered out the windows as their coach rolled through the dusty main street of the little frontier town. The men of the town wore the broad-brimmed hats that Jed associated with cowboys, and they all wore guns on their belts. "Welcome to the West!" Pa said.

When they reached the Double-L, the driver helped unload their luggage onto the porch of the large ranch house. "Welcome to the Double-L!" a cheery voice called from behind them, and the boys spun around to see a tall, thin man wearing denim trousers, a red-checkered shirt, and dusty cowboy boots. He took off an enormous hat, revealing a thick shock of unruly gray hair. Grinning broadly, he extended a strong, callused hand to Nathan. "Put 'er there, pardner!" he commanded. "I'm Will Laramy, an old friend of your Pa's. And you must be Nathan!" The boy returned the handshake.

As Jed shook hands with the tall, friendly man, he noticed the twinkle in the deep blue eyes, the deep laugh wrinkles etched around the corners of the man's eyes, and the magnificent white teeth displayed in the wide, wide smile. He decided immediately that he liked Mr. Laramy.

"You must be Jedediah," the man said warmly. "Heard about you. Glad to have you here, Son!" He grabbed Pa and hugged him, then shook hands with Mr. Phelps.

Mrs. Laramy turned out to be a short, heavy woman and Jed couldn't help contrasting her to her thin husband. She had the same friendly eyes and bright smile as Mr. Laramy. She was drying her hands on a bright gingham apron as she hurried out onto the porch to meet her guests. "Come in, come in," she chirped merrily, in a voice that reminded Jed of a meadowlark's song. "Do make yourselves at home!"

They walked inside with their host and hostess. The roughhewn walls of the ranch house looked strange to Jed after living in the Cartwright mansion. Mr. Laramy helped carry their luggage as he showed them to their rooms. Jed and Nathan would be staying right across the hall from Pa and Mr. Phelps.

A bell began to clang, and Mr. Laramy turned to his guests. "You arrived just in time!" he smiled. "That's the call for chow!" He led the way to a large dining room.

After the meal, Pa followed the boys to their room. "I'll be meeting with some ranchers tomorrow," he told them. "Mr. Laramy has told me to give you free run of his ranch. We can ask Mrs. Laramy in the morning what the meal schedule is. You'll be doing your schoolwork in the mornings with Mr. Phelps, but your afternoons are free. You are allowed to explore around the ranch, or even go into town, but I would prefer that you always stay together any time you are away from the Double-L."

The big man turned toward the door. "Goodnight, boys," he said softly. "I'll see you tomorrow night at chowtime." He closed the door, and both boys were asleep almost before their heads hit the pillows.

The next morning, Jed awoke and looked around the room. He frowned, then suddenly remembered. *We're at the Double-L Ranch! We've reached Hard Luck!* Jed woke Nathan, and the two boys hurriedly dressed, then slipped into the dining room. Mrs. Laramy had breakfast ready.

"Yore Pa already took off," she told the boys. "He said he'll be back in time for supper." Mr. Phelps entered the dining room just then, and the trio enjoyed breakfast with Mrs. Laramy.

The morning went quickly. Mr. Phelps and the boys were glad to do the schoolwork in a room that did not sway and bounce. "It's a little easier to write when you're not sitting in a moving stagecoach," Nathan remarked.

At lunch, Mr. Phelps addressed his pupils. "You're finished with school for the day," he told them. "I'm going to go to my room and read for a while, so I guess you two are on your own. But try to stay out of trouble."

When the meal was over, the boys walked out on the front porch of the ranch house. "Want to head in and look around town for a while?" Jed asked.

"Suppose so," Nathan answered. "Let's go tell Mrs. Laramy where we're going."

It was just a short walk to the main street of the little town. As the boys walked along the wooden sidewalk, Nathan spotted a whitewashed sign hanging over the street. "Blacksmith," he read. "I've never seen inside a blacksmith shop."

"You've never watched them make horseshoes and stuff?"

Jed replied. "Come on! I'll show you!"

The boys peeked in through the open door and spotted a big man hard at work beside a roaring fire. Jed pointed out the giant bellows that fed air to the fire, and explained how the fire could be made hot enough to soften iron. The man pulled a glowing, red-hot piece of iron from the furnace and began to strike it with a large hammer. Sparks flew as the metal took the shape the blacksmith desired.

"Hey! What are you guys doing?" a voice called, and Jed and Nathan turned, startled. A boy about their age walked toward them. His freckled face was one big, friendly grin. "I'm Seth!" he smiled, as he held out his hand. "Seth Olson. My father is the blacksmith."

The brothers shook hands with the friendly boy. "I'm Jed Cartwright," he said, "and this is my brother, Nathan."

"I want you to meet my father," Seth said as he led the way inside the shop. He walked over to the big anvil where the man was working. "Pa," he said, "I want you to meet some friends of mine. This is Ned, and this is Nathan."

"My name is Jed," the Cartwright boy corrected.

The sweating man nodded briefly. "Good to meet you, boys, but as you can see, I'm very busy right now. Sorry I can't stop to chat. But, you're welcome to stay and look around."

He turned to his son. "Seth, make sure that I have plenty of firewood," he said, "then you're free to go with your new friends. But be sure you're back and have your chores done before dark."

The three boys walked down the street of the little town together. "Where are you fellows from?" Seth asked. "I never saw you in town before."

"We're from St. Louis," Jed informed the boy. "Our Pa is

here on business for a couple of weeks, so we came with him."

"Don't you fellows go to school?" Seth asked.

"Yes, but we have a tutor for this trip," Jed answered, "cause we wanted to come with Pa. We'll be back in school when we get back to St. Louis."

The boys walked by a saloon just as a drunk came staggering out. As they watched, the man stumbled along the boardwalk, singing loudly. He grabbed at a hitching post, lost his balance, and fell on his face in the dust. Seth turned to the Cartwrights in disgust. "This saloon is open all the time now!" he said. "My Pa says that booze is a curse upon mankind." He turned around, and started back the way they had come. "Come on! I'll show you where I live."

Jed and Nathan followed Seth to the back of the blacksmith shop. "We live right behind Pa's shop," the friendly boy explained, "but we may not get to live here much longer." His cheerful face suddenly became sad.

Jed looked at him curiously. "Why not?" he asked.

"We owe Mr. Abernathy a lot of money," Seth answered. "Pa was sick for almost a year and couldn't do much work. We borrowed money from Mr. Abernathy, and now he has something called a mortgage on our house. If we don't pay him back pretty soon, he's gonna take our house away! And Pa's shop, too. He has the mortgage on that, too."

"Who is Mr. Abernathy?" Nathan asked.

"He's the banker," the other boy explained. "My Pa says that he's the tightest man this side of the Rocky Mountains!"

"How can he take your house away?" Nathan asked.

"When Pa borrowed the money, he signed a paper saying that Mr. Abernathy gets the house and shop if Pa can't pay the money back," Seth explained. "And we only have three more weeks to pay it!"

"Pa could loan him the money!" Nathan said to Jed.

Their new friend shook his head sadly. "I don't think so," he said. "Pa owes eighty dollars!"

The trio had reached Seth's house. As they walked up the porch steps, Seth suddenly cried out, "Look out!"

Jed whirled, but he was too late. A large, shaggy billy goat came flying around the corner of the house and butted him from behind, knocking him on his face. Jed jumped to his feet, but the goat disappeared as fast as he had come. Nathan doubled over with laughter, but Jed didn't think it was funny.

"I'm sorry about that!" Seth said to Jed. "That stupid goat does that every time! You learn to watch out for him."

The boys went into the little house. A large woman in a wrinkled dress appeared in the doorway, wiping her hands on her dress. Her dark hair was pulled back tightly into a bun. "Don't be carrying on and making a lot of noise!" she snapped at Seth. "I'll wallop you if you do!" She disappeared back through the doorway.

Seth turned toward the door. "Let's go out to the barn," he whispered to Jed and Nathan.

"I thought she was going to whip us all!" Jed remarked to Seth when they were in the safety of the barn. "Is your Ma always that mean?"

"She's not my Ma!" the other boy quickly protested. "That's Aunt Lou. She's Pa's sister. She's been living with us for almost a year now, and Ma says that all she does is make life miserable for all of us. She criticizes Pa all the time, but he won't stand up to her. She's older than Pa is, and I guess she always bossed him around when they were kids.

"You should see how strong she is!" the boy went on. "She can throw a bale of hay farther than Pa. She's never been married, and I think you can see why. I just try to stay out of her way."

The boys played in the haymow for a while, laughing and tumbling in the hay. They engaged in wrestling matches, and the loser always got his shirt stuffed with the prickly hay. Finally, Nathan pulled his watch from his pocket and looked at it. "We'd better be going," he said to Jed.

The boys turned to Seth. "It was fun getting to know you," Jed told their new friend. "How about if we come over to-morrow afternoon?"

Seth nodded eagerly. "As long as Pa doesn't have too much for me to do," he agreed. "And if I can get away from Aunt Lou."

The three boys strolled out of the barn, slapped each other on the back, and then it happened again. Jed suddenly was struck from behind and found himself lying face down in a pile of dirty straw. As he got up, he was furious. "That stupid goat!" he hollered. He turned around, but the billy goat was already gone. Seth and Nathan were both howling with laughter.

"I'm sorry, Jed; you'll have to watch out for that ol' goat," Seth snickered. He wiped the tears of laughter from his eyes. "See you tomorrow!"

The two brothers hurried home. "Sorry for laughing at you, Jed," Nathan apologized, "but that was funny!"

"I'm glad you enjoyed it!" Jed muttered darkly. "Next time, it's your turn!" He glanced at Nathan. "I'd sure hate to see Seth and his family lose their home," he commented. "Do you really think Pa would help them out?"

Nathan nodded. "You don't know Pa yet!" he said. "There's nothing he would rather do than help somebody in trouble. I think he would help the Olsons if he knew they were going to lose their home."

"Mr. Olson will lose his shop, too!" Jed remarked. "I sure hope we can help them, because three weeks isn't much time."

Gold Fever

The boys hiked back to the Double-L. Mrs. Laramy met them at the door with Wolf at her heels. "Yore Pa's not back yet," she informed them, "but he should be here any minute."

She opened the door wider, and Wolf pushed past her and sprang at Jed. The boy hugged the big dog. "Sorry you couldn't go today," he told Wolf, "but I think you can go with us tomorrow."

The boys heard a shout, and Pa came riding into the yard. The big man handed a large package down to Jed, and the boys eagerly tore it open. They found two fancy western hats and two pairs of expensive boots. "Thanks, Pa!" both boys said enthusiastically.

At supper that evening, the boys told their Pa about the Olsons, and the predicament that the family was facing. "Do you think we could help them, Pa?" Nathan pleaded. "They seem like nice people, but Mr. Abernathy is going to take their house!"

Pa looked at his plate thoughtfully. "We'll see," he said finally. "I'll have a talk with Mr. Olson."

Nathan then told the adults about Jed's experience with

the goat, and everyone at the table had a good laugh. Everyone, that is, but Jed.

When the meal was over, Pa smiled at Mrs. Laramy. "Fine meal, Adelia," he said. "The boys and I appreciate your hospitality."

He stood up and turned to the boys. "I'll be back in half an hour or so," he told them. "Maybe we can go riding together before dark."

Jed jumped to his feet. "I'll go with you!" Together the father and son walked into town. Jed showed Pa the way to the blacksmith shop, and they slipped through the narrow alley and knocked on the door of the small house behind the shop. The tall blacksmith came to the door.

"Mr. Olson?" Pa asked. The other man nodded. Pa held out his hand. "I'm Jake Cartwright. My boys met your son Seth today. May I talk with you a moment?"

The blacksmith stepped out on the porch, glanced at Jed, then looked back to Mr. Cartwright. "Sure," he said. "What's on your mind?" He gestured toward the door. "We could go inside."

Pa shook his head. "We'll just be a minute." He told the man what the boys had told him about Mr. Abernathy and the mortgage. "Is it true," Pa asked, "that you could lose your home and shop in just three weeks?"

Mr. Olson nodded. "Seth shouldn't have said anything," he said, "but, yes, it's true. Right now, I've got more work than I can handle, but the note comes due in three weeks! There's no way we can make that deadline!" The man struck his fist against his other hand. "We're about to lose everything!" he said dejectedly. "Everything I've worked for all these years!"

"I'd be glad to help you out," Pa offered. "I sure hate to

see Mr. Abernathy get your place here."

Mr. Olson shook his head. "Thanks, Mr. Cartwright," he replied, "but we ain't about to take charity!"

"How about a loan, then?" Pa offered. "No interest, just pay it back as you can."

The blacksmith shook his head again. "That still amounts to charity," he said. "Thanks, but we just can't accept that!" He held out his hand to Pa. "I do appreciate your offer to help, but I couldn't live with myself if I accepted."

Pa and Jed said goodnight and headed back to the ranch. Nathan had three horses saddled and came riding out to meet them, leading two mounts for Jed and Pa. Mr. Cartwright took the reins of the large, gray mare, leaving Jed with a small, white filly.

"Thanks, Son," Pa said, as he swung into the saddle. "Let's ride up into Dead Man's Canyon," he suggested. "I think you boys will like it up there."

"Dead Man's Canyon?" the boys echoed.

Pa laughed. "Well, I don't think they call it that any more, but that's what we used to call it years ago!" he explained. "I think they call it Weaver's Canyon now. My uncle lived in Hard Luck when I was in my teen years, and I stayed with him one summer. My cousins and I spent hours and hours in Dead Man's Canyon, exploring all the caves."

He rode away with the boys following. They took a trail that led up into the foothills above the town, then followed a crystal clear stream that flowed out of a rugged box canyon.

Jed looked up at the sheer canyon walls above them. "This is beautiful!" he exclaimed. "Bet you couldn't climb those canyon walls, could you?"

Pa shook his head. "The only way into the canyon is the way we came," he said. "The other end of the canyon is a precipice nearly a thousand feet high."

Nathan pointed. "Look! There's a cave!" he shouted.

Pa nodded. "There's heaps of them in this canyon," he replied. "Most of them aren't very deep, but a couple of them run clear under the mountain."

The sun was setting over the western edge of the canyon, and the trio sat silently on their mounts, watching the brilliant display of colors. Finally, Pa turned his horse around on the narrow trail. "We'd better head home, boys," he called. "It's getting dark, fast!"

The next morning, Jed woke Nathan. "Let's get our schoolwork done as fast as we can today," he suggested. "Maybe Mr. Phelps will let us go early! We'll see if Seth wants to explore the canyon with us!"

The boys worked hard at their schoolwork, but Mr. Phelps wouldn't release them until lunchtime. When Mrs. Laramy heard of their plans to explore the canyon, she insisted on packing them a lunch. "Why stay and eat in this stuffy house?" she laughed as she handed Nathan a cloth sack and a tin canteen of water. "Go up and enjoy yoreselves in the canyon. But be careful!"

The boys thanked her, whistled for Wolf, then headed into town.

Seth wasn't at the blacksmith shop, so they walked around to the house in back. "Watch out for that stupid goat!" Jed muttered, as they knocked on the door. But the goat was nowhere in sight, and Jed relaxed a little.

Seth opened the door at their second knock. "I'll be with you in a few minutes," he said. "Ma has me doin' some chores."

Wolf came around the corner of the house just then, and the boy's eyes widened in astonishment. "Look at the size of that dog!" he exclaimed. "He's bigger than a wolf!"

Jed laughed. "He's mine!" he told his friend proudly. "And his name is Wolf."

Just then, the old billy goat charged around the opposite corner of the house and headed straight for Jed. The boy found himself lying in the grass beside the porch steps. The goat disappeared around the corner of the house with the big dog at his heels.

"Get him, Wolf!" Jed called to the dog. "Maybe you can teach him to leave me alone!" He picked up his new hat from the ground and dusted it off. "I hate that goat!" he fumed. Seth and Nathan were both biting their lips to keep from laughing.

When the chores were finished, the boys headed back to the Double-L for some horses. Jed told Seth about Dead Man's Canyon. "Never heard of it," Seth replied.

The boys saddled three horses and headed for the canyon. Jed led the way, with Wolf running alongside his horse. When they reached the canyon, Seth began to laugh.

"This is Weaver's Canyon!" he said. "I never heard anyone call it 'Dead Man's Canyon' before!" He rode forward. "Wait until you see the waterfall at the other end," he called. "It's fantastic!"

The boys rode down the narrow trail on the canyon floor, following the stream that flowed through the canyon. Again, Jed marveled at the rugged beauty of the place. An eagle circled high overhead, riding the warm air currents that floated upward. As they neared a rock wall at the end of the canyon, Seth pointed. "You'll see it just around the bend!" he called.

The horses slipped through a narrow cleft in the rock, and Jed realized that the canyon did not end where it had seemed to. It continued for another quarter mile or so, and ended in a spectacular eighty-foot waterfall.

The boys spent the afternoon exploring some of the caves they found. Most did not go in very far, but one or two continued until the boys were afraid of being lost in the darkness. "We'll have to bring lanterns tomorrow," Seth said as they rode home.

As they entered town, a wild-eyed man came riding down the dusty main street, firing a revolver into the air. "Gold!" he screamed. "They found gold!"

People came running from everywhere to see what was going on. The stores and bank were suddenly without customers as the crowd in the street grew. Even the saloon was empty. The people thronged the man as he leaped from his winded horse.

"They found gold!" the man cried again. "Out on Clifford's Creek! There's nuggets the size of potatoes!" He threw his hat into the air and fired his revolver at it. "It's gold! This will make Sutter's Mill look like a Sunday school picnic!"

The crowd went crazy. Men, women, and children dashed in the direction of Clifford's Creek. Others turned back into town and got their horses or buggies, then joined in the mad race. The boys reined their horses to the side of the street as people surged past them. They had never seen people in such frenzy. Wolf barked and barked at all the excitement.

An old man standing on the boardwalk near the boys sadly shook his head. "Gold fever!" he said to the boys, stroking his long, gray beard. "Gold fever. I've seen it strike afore, and it ain't healthy. Folks will be dead afore this is over."

Seth dismounted, said good-bye, and hurried home to tell his father what had happened. Jed and Nathan sat on their horses, watching the little town. Jed held the reins to the horse

Seth had ridden.

The town was empty. One or two old-timers still sat in their rocking chairs on the porches, but everyone else was gone, caught up in the mad dash for Clifford's Creek.

"Should we go out to Clifford's Creek?" Nathan asked, but Jed shook his head.

"We'd better ask Pa first," he said. "People were acting mighty crazy! It could be dangerous out there!"

The boys rode out to the Double-L and took care of their horses, then headed into the ranch house. Pa came in about an hour later. The boys started to tell him about the gold strike, but he just nodded his head sadly.

"I know," he said. "Gold fever! Three men are dead already, because of gold fever! One man found a nugget just a short while ago, and five men tried to claim it. When the bullets stopped flying, three men were dead!"

He looked at the boys. "Jed, Nathan, you are not to go anywhere near Clifford's Creek, unless I'm with you! It's not going to be a safe place to be until this gold fever has died out!"

The next afternoon, when school was finished, the boys walked into town. The streets were strangely empty. The stores, bank, and saloon were all closed, and an eerie silence prevailed. Gold fever had struck the town of Hard Luck.

Panning For Gold

Several days went by, and the flurry of excitement over gold finally began to wane. A few nuggets had been found, along with small quantities of gold dust, but most people found nothing. Several more people had been killed in the disputes that erupted in the search for the precious metal.

The undertaker was busier than usual, and Mr. Olson's blacksmith shop kept him busy from morning till night as the gold-seekers demanded tools and equipment, but very few people actually profited from the gold strike on Clifford's Creek.

Slowly, life in Hard Luck returned to normal. When most of the furor had died away, Mr. Cartwright took Jed and Nathan out to the place where the gold strike had taken place. There were still a number of prospectors searching the creek for the elusive yellow metal.

Men were standing in the shallow water, shoveling sand and gravel into long, narrow sluice boxes. As the water flowed through the boxes, the men rocked them from side to side and watched the bottom slats eagerly, hoping to spot a speck of the shiny metal. Other men shoveled sand and gravel into wide, shallow tin pans. Holding the pans at an angle in the current, they would swish the creek water around in the pan, washing the sand and gravel back out.

"That's called 'panning,' " Pa said. "Any gold in the gravel will sink to the bottom of the pan because it's heavier, and hopefully stay in the pan as the sand and gravel are washed out."

As they rode along the creek bank, a prospector called to them, "Hey, lads, I'm ready for a break! Care to try your hand at panning for gold?"

Nathan looked up at Pa. "Could we?"

Pa smiled and nodded. "I don't think it will hurt," he said. "But, don't expect to find too much."

Both boys snatched off their new boots and waded eagerly into the creek. The man handed the shovel to Nathan and the pan to Jed. "Keep the pan at an angle, like this," he said, dipping the upstream edge of the pan into the water slightly. "But, don't let the water fill the pan too quickly."

He sat on the edge of the stream and watched as the boys tried their hand at panning—Nathan with the shovel and Jed with the pan. After a few minutes, the boys switched places. Jed dumped a shovelful of sand and gravel into the pan, and Nathan swished the pan in the water.

As he brought the pan out of the water, he screamed, "I got one! It's the size of a hen's egg!"

Men came running from all directions. The man who owned the tools leaped into the water. "It's mine!" he hollered. "It's mine! You found it on my claim!"

Nathan reached into the pan and plucked the object out. He held it in the air. "It's the size of a hen's egg all right! But, it's just a rock!" He laughed at the excitement he had created with his little joke.

The owner jerked the pan roughly from Nathan's hands. "Git out of here, boy!" he snarled. "We ain't got no time for such foolishness!"

The boys quickly splashed out of the water and pulled on their boots. Prospectors all around them were still giving them dirty looks. "Let's get out of here, boys!" Pa suggested. They mounted and rode away from Clifford's Creek.

"Those men couldn't even take a little joke!" Nathan complained. "I thought that the owner of the pan was going to kill me when he thought I had a nugget!"

Pa nodded. "Gold is a strange thing, boys. People will kill for it. And yet, when you do find gold, you also find that it doesn't make you happy."

At supper that evening, Pa told the story of Nathan's "nugget." The adults laughed and laughed at the joke the boy had played on the prospectors. "I'm just glad one of them didn't shoot you, Nathan," Mr. Laramy said, wiping his eyes.

"I'm going to be gone for a few days," Pa announced. He turned to his sons. "Be sure to do your school work, just as Mr. Phelps tells you to. If you need anything, just ask Mr. or Mrs. Laramy. And stay away from Clifford's Creek."

Both boys nodded. "We will, sir!" they chorused together.

Pa left early the next morning. The boys awoke to find him already gone. Mr. Phelps ate breakfast with them, and then they started in on their schoolwork. After lunch, they headed into town.

"I've got some money," Jed told Seth and Nathan as they sat in the swing on the Olson's porch. "Let's go down to the general store and see if they have any molasses candy." The other boys agreed, and the three set off eagerly.

"Look out!" Nathan called, but once again, Jed found himself on the ground. He leaped to his feet, but the goat was nowhere in sight. "Why does he always pick me?" Jed fumed. He caught the twinkle in Nathan's eyes. "It's not funny!" he stormed. "Why doesn't he ever butt you?"

When they reached the store, Jed and Nathan paused in the doorway, but Seth hurried inside. "Look at this!" he called, and the others hurried over to him. "Watch now!" Seth held a little wooden clown in his hand, which he set on the top rung of a six-inch wooden ladder. The little ladder was vertical, with the bottom secured by a wooden base. When the boy released the little clown, the tiny figure tumbled from one rung to another, all the way down the ladder.

"It's a Tumbling Tommy," Nathan said. "I saw them once in St. Louis."

The boys played with the little wooden toy for several minutes. Suddenly Jed whispered, "Sh-h! Listen!"

Two men in the next aisle of the mercantile were talking in low voices. The boys crept over against the counter and stood quietly. They could make out most of what the men were saying.

"I still say that there's a lot of gold left in the Bluebird!" one man said. "Old Man Potter got that gold from somewhere!"

"Yeah, but that was thirty years ago!" a second voice replied.

"If it was there thirty years ago," the first voice spoke again, "then it's there now! Just think of it, all that gold just sittin' there, waitin' for someone to come along and claim it!"

"It ain't that easy!" the second voice argued again. "People around here looked for Jacob Potter's mine for years! And nobody ever found nuthin'!"

The boys looked at each other, wide-eyed. "What mine

do you think they're talking about?" Nathan whispered. Jed held up one hand to silence him, as the men were talking again.

"That's cause nobody ever found Potter's map!" the first voice said. "They say he made one, you know, before his brother came out from Philadelphy!"

"Then why didn't his brother find the mine?" the second voice asked.

Jed was wondering the same thing. The voice on the other side of the partition gave the answer. "Cause they shot Potter afore his brother got here! And nobody ever found his map! If we can find it, the gold is ours!"

Just then Seth leaned against a counter, and a small glass bottle crashed to the floor. The voices stopped at the sound, and there was the noise of scurrying feet. Jed hurried around the corner and peered down the aisle, but it was empty. The men were gone. The boys scrambled to the entrance of the store just in time to see the door swinging closed.

Together, they hurried out the door. But the street was empty. The owners of the voices had vanished. Disappointed, the boys went back into the store.

Later, back at Seth's house, the boys discussed the conversation they had overheard in the store. "We ought to look for the mine," Seth insisted. "If we could find it, we could keep our house and Pa's shop! I could pay Mr. Abernathy back with my share of the gold! Pa only has a little over two weeks left!"

"Where do you think the map is?" Nathan asked.

"The man said that it was never found," Jed answered. "But I think that Seth is right! We ought to look for it. We have as good a chance at finding it as anybody."

They discussed their ideas for finding the mine for several more minutes. Suddenly a voice boomed out, "Seth! Git me a bucket of water!"

The boys jumped and turned around. There in the doorway stood Aunt Lou. They had been so absorbed in discussing the mine that they hadn't even heard her approach. "Yes, Aunt Lou," Seth replied and hurried off to the well. The woman gave the Cartwright boys a cold look and bustled back inside the house.

Seth joined them again on the porch a minute or two later. "Let's get out of here!" he whispered, "before she thinks of some other chore for me to do!"

The boys hurried from the yard. Jed kept a sharp eye out behind him, but the belligerent old billy goat did not make an appearance. Seth laughed. "He only strikes when you're not watching, Jed," he chuckled.

Suddenly, Nathan had an idea. "Let's ask your Pa if he knows where Old Man Potter used to live," he suggested. "That would be the place to look for the map."

The boys hurried into the blacksmith shop. Mr. Olson was sitting on a three-legged stool, filing the edge of a mattock. He looked up as they entered. "Pa," Seth asked, "did you ever hear of a man named Jacob Potter?"

The man shook his head, then suddenly held up one finger. "Wait," he said, "yes, I have. Old Man Potter, they used to call him."

"Do you know where he lived?" Jed questioned.

The man turned to face him. "Can't say that I do, Jed," he answered. "Years ago I heard that he lived on Rushing Creek, close to where it joins Clifford's Creek, but I don't know if that was true or not. Of course, that was a long time ago."

Jed and Nathan turned and looked at each other excitedly. Perhaps they could find the old man's cabin!

"Why all the interest in Old Man Potter?" Mr. Olson asked suddenly. "Have you heard the legend of Old Man Potter and the Bluebird Gold Mine?"

The boys glanced at each other again, and Jed answered, "We just heard someone talking about the legend today. We were wondering who Old Man Potter was."

The man turned back to his work and the boys hurried from the shop. "You guys want to ride out to Rushing Creek?" Jed asked. "We could try to find Old Man Potter's cabin!"

Seth shook his head. "I don't dare go right now," he said. "I've gotta git started on my chores." He looked at the two brothers. "It's no use anyway," he said. "I've been out to Rushing Creek lots of times, hunting rabbits. There's not a cabin around there for miles! I think we'd just waste our time searching out there."

"See you later, Seth!" Nathan called out, as their friend hurried toward the house.

"Hey, Seth!" Jed called suddenly. "Watch out for the goat!" The boy spun around quickly, but there was no goat behind him. Both the Cartwrights laughed as they headed for the Double-L.

"Look!" Nathan whispered. "That man has a Bible." Jed looked in the direction that Nathan pointed, and saw a man sitting on the front porch of a small house, reading a Bible. He looked up as the boys approached.

"Howdy, lads!" he called out.

Jed stopped and leaned over the rail fence. "Are you a Christian?" he asked. "We noticed that you have a Bible."

"Yes, I am," the man smiled, as he walked toward the fence. He was short and stocky, with hair the color of cedar shavings and a face that was covered with freckles. "I'm Pastor Wood," he said, and held out a thick, freckled hand. The boys shook the man's hand and introduced themselves.

"It's good to meet you boys," Pastor Wood said. "And now, I'd like to ask you a question. Are you Christians?"

Jed nodded eagerly. "I am!" he said. "I got saved just a few weeks ago!"

The man turned to Nathan. "How about you, Son?"

Nathan nodded, too. "I got saved several years ago," he replied. "Did you say that you are a pastor? Where is your church?"

The man smiled again. "We're starting a church right here in my home!" he replied. "This town is very ungodly, and these people need the Lord. But, so far, not many people are coming to hear the Gospel."

He looked thoughtful. "My wife and I think that perhaps more people would come if we had a real church building, instead of meeting in our home. But, I don't think we'll ever have the money to build a church."

"We'll see if we can come Sunday," Jed promised as they walked away. "My Pa would like to meet you, too."

That night, Jed lay in bed, thinking. Finally, he turned over and whispered, "Hey, Nathan! Are you still awake?"

"I am now!" his brother whispered. "What's on your mind?"

"We're gonna find the Bluebird Gold Mine!" Jed told his brother. "I just know it! And I know what I'm gonna do with my share of the gold. I'm gonna give it to Pastor Wood, so he can build his church!"

"I know what Seth is going to do with his share of the gold," Nathan said. "After he helps his Pa pay off the mortgage, he wants to get a horse! He wants one so badly, I almost think he'd steal one!"

Jed lay quietly for a few minutes, thinking about what

they had heard in the store that day. "Let's go out to Rushing Creek tomorrow," he whispered, "and see if we can find Old Man Potter's cabin!" But Nathan had again fallen asleep.

The Search

The next afternoon Jed and Nathan saddled up and rode into town. Nathan led an extra horse for Seth. When they reached the Olson house, Seth met them on the porch.

"I can't go with you today," he called out sadly when he saw his friends. "Ma has a ton of chores for me to do. It will probably take me two or three hours."

Jed dismounted. "We'll help you," he said brightly. "The three of us can get your chores done in no time."

Seth looked doubtful. "I don't know," he said. "There's an awful lot to do."

But the boys led their horses to the Olson barn and pitched in with Seth. Wolf disappeared behind the barn while they worked. An hour or so later, they were finished.

A slender woman with a pleasant, friendly-looking face came to the door. She smiled at Jed and Nathan. "I'm Mrs. Olson," she said. "I'm Seth's mother."

She turned to her son. "You can go with your friends, now," she told him, "but be home before dark."

The boys raced to the barn and quickly fetched the horses. "I didn't see your goat today!" Jed commented. He whistled for Wolf.

With Seth leading the way, the boys rode toward Rushing Creek. A few minutes later, they reined in on the bank of a swift, noisy creek. The water was clear and inviting as it tumbled forcefully along in its rocky bed. "This is it," Seth called to his companions. "Rushing Creek! We'll follow it downstream to where it meets up with Clifford's Creek. But, I don't remember seeing a cabin anywhere along here."

"The cabin may be gone now," Jed reminded him. "Remember, it was thirty years ago that Old Man Potter lived around here." The boys rode downstream, again with Seth in the lead. They zigzagged back and forth through the brush, searching for the cabin, but finding nothing.

Suddenly, Seth's horse reared up in panic, his forelegs slashing the air, his nostrils flared in terror. The boy grabbed frantically at the saddle horn. His face went white with fear. The horse reared again, and Seth dropped the reins.

Jed leaped from his saddle and dashed to the side of the frightened horse. He leaped high and caught the horse's bridle. But the horse reared again, lifting Jed completely off the ground.

"It's all right!" Jed called to the horse. He hung on bravely, and the horse finally lowered his forelegs to the ground. But the big animal still stamped nervously.

Nathan spotted the reason for the horse's strange behavior. "It's a rattler!" he called to Jed. "Over to your right! Lead the horse to the left, away from the snake!"

Jed quickly followed his brother's instructions, and the horse calmed down, once he was away from the rattlesnake. Jed glanced up at Seth. His face was still pale, and he was trembling.

The boy managed a weak grin at Jed. "Thanks!" he said.

"That was close!"

Jed picked up a stout branch and used it to kill the snake. Looping the body of the dead reptile over the branch, he carried it to the edge of the creek and flung it in. "That's the end of that rattler!" he laughed triumphantly as he dropped the branch.

Jed remounted and turned to Seth. "Care to go on?"

Seth nodded nervously. "Why don't one of you ride ahead of me, though," he suggested. "I don't want to meet up with any more rattlers!"

The boys continued their search downstream. They reached the point where Rushing Creek emptied into Clifford's Creek, but had found no sign of a cabin anywhere. They rode in large circles throughout the area of the junction of the two creeks, again finding nothing. Jed even forded the creek with his horse and rode along the other side, but saw no sign of any buildings.

Finally, the three boys brought their horses together for a conference. Jed and Seth were discouraged, but Nathan had a suggestion. "We've been looking for a standing building," he said. "Perhaps the building is gone, or most of it, anyway. Let's ride back upstream, a little slower this time. Look for the remains of a foundation, the pit from an outhouse, or something that would tell us that there used to be a cabin there."

The other boys agreed. "Maybe we just didn't look close enough," Seth said.

They rode back upstream, watching the ground closely. They circled through the tall weeds, checking anything that suggested a rectangular foundation. Just a few hundred yards upstream, Jed stopped his horse and dismounted. "Hey, fellows, look at this!" he called.

Nathan and Seth rode over eagerly. Jed was kicking the

toe of his boot into the dirt at the edge of a large, square stone half-buried in the ground. "Do you think this could have been the corner of the foundation for a cabin?" he asked as they rode up.

Both boys dismounted quickly. Nathan looked carefully at the large stone, then went shuffling through the tall grass. A moment or two later, he found a second stone, similar to the first. "Look at this!" he called. "Here's another one of them!"

The boys searched through the weeds and found two more. The four stones formed a rectangle, roughly twelve by sixteen feet. Jed threw his hat into the air. "We found it!" he cried excitedly. "This has to be Old Man Potter's cabin!"

The Old Well

There was nothing left of the little cabin but the four large stones that had supported the floor timbers of the building. Jed and Nathan tried digging in the dirt beneath where the cabin floor had been, but the ground was hard and unyielding.

Suddenly, Seth called out, "Hey, Jed! Come look at this!"

Jed ran over to him. Seth had been wandering through the weeds some forty feet from where the building had stood. He had discovered a ring of large stones, half-buried in the ground. The center of the ring was a mound of molding leaves and rotting timbers.

Seth looked up as Jed approached. "What do you think it was?" he asked.

Jed recognized the shape immediately. "It's an old well!" he shouted.

Seth shook his head. "The creek's right here, close by," he pointed out. "Why would he have a well?"

Jed shrugged. "I don't know," he answered. "The creek's not very big. Maybe it goes dry part of the year."

Nathan came over to see what the excitement was all about. Seth showed him their find. "It's an old well," he told Nathan.

Jed jumped into the center of the circle, and the fill sank several inches beneath his weight. He climbed back out. "It's not solid," he told the others. "Maybe we can dig it out!"

"What do we want to do that for?" Nathan asked.

Jed shrugged. "I don't know," he answered. "I just think we should see what was in it! Sometimes people even hid their valuables in their well! Maybe Potter hid his gold in this one!"

"It's just an old well!" Seth declared, but the boys got down and began to dig with their hands anyway. The fill was not at all solid, and the digging progressed rapidly. Wolf lay on the ground with his head on his paws, watching the proceedings. Soon, Nathan was standing in a waist-deep hole, handing material up to the others to remove. Finally, Seth looked up at the sky.

"We'd better go," he said, "or we'll all be in trouble! We can dig here again tomorrow."

He and Jed helped pull Nathan out of the hole, as the well was now as deep as the boy was tall. "We'll need a shovel, a bucket, and a rope," Seth decided.

Jed looked at his companions. "Not a word about this to anyone, right? Not even Mr. and Mrs. Laramy!"

Seth nodded in agreement. "I won't even tell Pa yet," he said.

The boys mounted their horses and rode quickly toward Hard Luck, excited about their find. Perhaps there was nothing in the old well, but at least they were reasonably sure that they had located the site for Old Man Potter's cabin. At the Olson house, Seth dismounted and handed the reins of his horse to Jed. "See you tomorrow!" he called as he hurried into the house.

The next morning, a light rain was falling when the boys got up. Jed wiped the fog from the window and looked out anxiously. "Hope it doesn't rain all day!" he said to Nathan.

The boys could hardly sit still during their schoolwork with Mr. Phelps. They were eager to get back up to Old Man Potter's cabin. Finally, the man threw up his hands in desperation. "I don't know where your minds are today," he sputtered, "but they're not on grammar or arithmetic! Why don't we stop early today, and we can hit it hard again tomorrow."

The boys grinned at each other, but the grins disappeared as the man warned, "But don't think you're getting out of anything! This only means you'll have to work harder tomorrow!"

Mrs. Laramy was surprised to learn that the boys were finished early. "We're not going to eat for another hour," she said. "Why don't I pack you a quick lunch, and you can take it with you. I don't know what you lads are up to, but I can tell that you're in a hurry to be off and running. Sit down, and I'll have a lunch ready to carry in three minutes!"

The rain was still falling gently, so Nathan put on a poncho and went out to the barn to saddle the horses while Jed waited in the kitchen for the lunches. Sure enough, in no time at all the kind woman handed him a small cloth sack. "There's enough food in there to feed a small army," she said, "but don't waste any!" Jed thanked her and hurried to the barn.

Nathan had a forty-foot coil of hemp rope hanging on his saddle. He handed Jed a large tin bucket. "You carry this," he told Jed, "and I'll carry the shovel!"

Minutes later, the boys knocked on the Olson's door, and Aunt Lou answered their knock. "He's over at the shop," she said coldly when she saw them, "but why don't you just leave him alone? His Pa doesn't want you botherin' him!" She closed the door abruptly.

The boys tied the three horses to a mesquite tree in the yard, then walked across to the shop. Jed heard a sound behind him but before he could turn, the goat had butted him and knocked him against the wall of the blacksmith shop. Jed seized a large rock and turned, ready to hurl it at the goat, but again, the crafty animal had run away. Jed flung the rock to the ground, then hurried into the shop after Nathan.

Seth was stoking the furnace with wood when the boys entered. He turned as they came in. "I can't go today, fellows," he called when he saw them. "Pa says I'm gonna be busy all day!" He threw a chunk of wood into the furnace and came over to them.

"Let me know if you find anything important!" he begged in a whisper. "Hopefully, I can go tomorrow. But Pa says he's covered up today and needs my help."

"Can we put the extra horse in your barn till we get back?" Jed asked. "That will save taking her back home now."

Mr. Olson heard him and waved his hand. "No problem, Jed," he replied, "you can put her in Black's old stall."

The Cartwright boys rode toward Rushing Creek. Wolf raced ahead as if he knew exactly where they were going. When they reached the site of the cabin they tied their horses securely to a mesquite. The rain had slowed to a drizzle, and the sun was trying determinedly to escape from behind the clouds.

Jed tied one end of the rope to a scrub pine and dropped the other end into the well. "I'll dig first!" he offered. "When the bucket is full, you pull the rope up and empty it over there."

The boy lowered himself down the rope. Nathan dropped the bucket and shovel to him, and Jed tied one end of the rope to the handle of the bucket. Nathan sat on the edge of the well and watched as Jed worked. When the bucket was full, Jed set the shovel down.

"Haul away!" he called to his brother. "One load of junk, coming up!" Nathan emptied the bucket and dropped it into the old well again.

The boys decided to switch places every twenty bucket loads. The debris was easy to clear, and in less than two hours they were nearly fifteen feet down. Nathan was working in the well, and his brother was busily carving a cactus wren for Mrs. Laramy in between bucket loads.

As Jed emptied the bucket, Nathan rested in the bottom of the well shaft. "Hey! Look at this!" he suddenly called.

Jed ran back and knelt at the edge of the hole. "What is it?" he called down. His voice echoed in the shaft. The hole was now so deep that it was dark at the bottom. Jed could see Nathan's face, but nearly everything else was just dark shadows.

"It's some kind of pipe, stuck in between the rocks in the side wall of the well!" Nathan hollered up. His voice had a hollow, spooky sound as it floated up out of the deep shaft.

"Oh." Jed was disappointed. "I thought maybe you had found something important!"

"I'm gonna try to get it out!" Nathan called. He chipped away at the side of the well with the blade of the shovel. He was able to pry a couple of the rocks loose, then dig the earth away from the pipe. Finally, he pried the pipe out of the wall.

"It's just an old, iron pipe," he called up to Jed. "It's about a foot long!"

"What's it for?" Jed hollered down.

"I don't know," Nathan replied. "But both ends are plugged closed with mud or something. Lower the bucket!

I'll send it up."

Jed sent the bucket swinging down into the well. Nathan dropped the old pipe into it and jerked on the rope. "Haul away!" he called.

Jed dropped the length of rusty pipe on the ground and sent the bucket back to Nathan, who picked up the shovel and started digging again. Jed returned to his carving. The boys worked for another twenty minutes or so, until Nathan called, "Let's break for lunch! I'm hungry!" Hand over hand, he climbed the rope out of the well.

The boys prayed over the lunch, opened the sack that Mrs. Laramy had sent, and bit into roast beef sandwiches. "Mmm," Jed said, munching on his sandwich, "ever notice how good food tastes when you eat outdoors?"

He eyed the rusty pipe lying on the ground, then picked it up. "Look at this, Nate! Both ends of the pipe are plugged up with . . . it looks like—beeswax! Why would anyone plug up the ends of an old pipe and drive it into the wall of a well?"

Jed pulled his knife from his pocket and dug at the wax. "It's hard as a rock! Betcha it's thirty years old!" He took another bite of the sandwich and continued to dig at the wax. When he had made a hole big enough, he inserted his finger and tugged at the wax plug. Finally, it began to move, then popped free.

Jed looked into the pipe. "It's just an old piece of moldy leather, all rolled up! This is strange!" He tapped the pipe sharply against the trunk of the pine tree, and the leather roll slid from the iron tube. Jed unrolled the leather carefully.

Nathan scooted over to see the moldy leather object. There were strange markings on the leather, drawn in a dark brown ink. Two heavy, parallel lines crossed the center of the leather horizontally. Between the parallel lines was a crude drawing of what appeared to be a river, and, just below it, a large capital "M" was scrawled. Mountains were drawn on each side of the two lines, and a dark "X" was drawn close to one line. In the bottom right hand corner were the letters "JP". Some of the markings were faded, but the boys could make most of them out.

"What is it?" Nathan asked.

"I don't know," Jed replied. He was just as puzzled as his brother was. He looked at Nathan. "Why would anyone hide an old piece of leather in a well? It doesn't make sense!"

They stared at the crude drawings for several minutes. Jed turned the leather over and looked at the back, but there was nothing on it. He carefully set the leather face up again in the grass.

"You know," he said, "it kinda looks like some sort of a . . ."

"Map!" both brothers said at the same instant. They looked at each other in delight.

"Nathan!" Jed shouted. "We found it! This is Old Man Potter's map to the Bluebird Gold Mine! This is the map he made for his brother!" He pointed to the letters down in the corner. "Look, Nate! JP! Jacob Potter! This must be the map! We found it! Wait till we tell Seth!"

The brothers thumped each other on the back in their excitement. They danced around in exhilaration, whooping with joy. Then they knelt in the grass and studied the old map again.

"What are these two lines running across the center of the map?" Nathan asked. "And what does the M stand for?"

"I don't know," Jed replied. He turned the map upside down. "Maybe this isn't an M. Maybe it's a W."

Nathan shook his head. "No," he said, "cause then the JP is upside down!"

Jed bent down with his face just inches from the leather. "Look

at this, Nate!" he said. He pointed to the right hand side of the
map, between the two heavy lines. "It's pretty faded, but isn't this
the letter C?"

Nathan squinted at the markings. "I think you're right!
But if JP stands for Jacob Potter, what does M stand for, and
what does C stand for?"

"Hey, look, Nathan!" Jed said suddenly. "What do these
wiggly lines across the center look like?"

"I think it's supposed to be water," the other boy replied.
"A river or a creek."

"That's what I think, too," Jed said. "Look how it runs
through the middle of the two parallel lines. If this is a river,
maybe the other two lines are supposed to be a canyon!"

"The X is drawn between the two lines," Nathan observed,
"so maybe the gold mine is in a canyon!"

Jed nodded. "Right, but which one? There must be hundreds of canyons around here."

The boys studied the old leather map for several more
minutes, but finally had to admit that they were no closer to
solving the mystery. Jed carefully rolled the old document up
and poked it back inside the pipe. "Let's show it to Seth, and
see what he thinks," he said. "Boy, wait until he hears that we
found the map!"

Jed stood up and whistled for Wolf, and the boys happily
mounted their horses for the trip back to town. As they neared
town, Jed tucked the pipe inside his shirt. "I don't want anyone except Seth to know that we have it!" he told his brother.

When they reached the blacksmith shop, Mr. Olson was
working alone. "Seth is over at the house, doing his chores,"
the burly blacksmith told them.

The Cartwrights quickly crossed over to the Olson house
and knocked briskly. Aunt Lou came to the door. "What do you

want?" she asked in a gruff voice.

"Can we see Seth?" Jed asked timidly. The big woman turned and went into the house, closing the door behind her. The boys turned to go, but the door suddenly popped open and Seth appeared.

"Hi, guys!" he greeted them cheerfully. "I can't talk long, but tell me—did you find anything?"

"You won't believe it," Jed said, his eyes sparkling, "but we found the map!" He pulled the pipe from his shirt. "It's in here!"

Seth's eyes grew wide. "Oh, wow!" he whispered. "Let's see it!"

The Old Map

Jed started to slide the roll of leather from the pipe, but as he did so, he happened to glance up toward the house. Aunt Lou stood in the doorway, her hands on her hips. She frowned when she realized that Jed had noticed her presence. "Why don't you git back to work, Seth!" she barked. "Yore Ma needs you!"

Jed quickly tucked the map back inside his shirt, hoping that the big woman hadn't seen what it was. "We'll show you tomorrow!" he whispered to Seth. As their friend headed back into the house, the brothers hurried to the barn to fetch the third horse.

"Let's just bring two horses tomorrow," Nathan suggested. "Two of us can ride double, and we won't be stuck with an extra horse if Seth can't come." He looked at Jed. "Do you think she saw the map?"

His brother shook his head. "I don't think so," he answered. "She was pretty mad at Seth, and I don't think she even noticed us!"

When the boys reached the safety of the Double-L barn, Jed hid the map under a pile of hay in the loft. "I wish Pa was back," he thought aloud. "I'd like to show the map to him."

After a supper of steaks and fresh vegetables, Mrs. Laramy served an apple pie for dessert. She noticed the restlessness of her young guests. "What are you boys so antsy about?" she asked. "I don't know what you lads are up to, but tonight you can hardly sit still! Nathan, you've hardly eaten a bite!"

The brothers looked at each other, and then at the adults around the table. All eyes were on them. "I'm sorry, Mrs. Laramy," Jed said quietly. "We're just wanting to get out and ride again."

"You two have spent so much time in the saddle lately," the woman observed, "you're gonna wear the horses out!"

The boys did their best to relax and enjoy the dessert. When the meal was finished, Jed stood up and followed Mrs. Laramy into the kitchen. "Can we help you with the dishes?" he asked, hoping for a negative answer.

The woman gave him a playful shove. "Jedediah!" she said, in mock astonishment, "dishes are women's work! You boys get out of here and go riding or something!"

The boys quickly disappeared from the house and headed to the barn. Nathan pulled the pipe from its hiding place and unrolled the map. Both brothers crouched over the old piece of leather, studying the strange markings intently.

"I think you were right!" Nathan said. "These lines in the middle are supposed to be a canyon. So the gold mine must be in a canyon! But, which one?"

Finally, they returned the old map to its hiding place and headed for bed. Both boys lay awake for a long time, puzzling over the mystery of the old map.

The next afternoon, they saddled two horses and headed for the Olson's. Seth was out on the porch. "I can go today!" he called when he saw the Cartwrights. He swung up behind

Jed's saddle. "Let's see the map!" he said eagerly.

Jed shook his head. "Wait until we're out of town, away from prying eyes!"

They rode out toward Rushing Creek. When they had left the houses and shops behind, Jed turned his horse from the trail and rode behind a large cholla cactus. The boys scrambled down from their mounts and Jed pulled the pipe from his shirt. He unrolled the leather map on the sand, and Seth fell to his knees eagerly.

Jed and Nathan explained their interpretation of the strange markings. They pointed out the river, the canyon, and the initials "JP." "But, we don't understand what the M and the C stand for," Nathan commented.

"Look at the funny little tail on the M," Jed said. "Why do you think he drew it that way?"

"I noticed that, too!" Nathan mentioned.

Seth pointed to a faint mark at the left side of the old map, placed between the parallel lines. "What letter is this?" he asked.

Both brothers leaned closer. "We didn't notice that!" Jed replied. "It's so faint we didn't even see it! It looks like a D or an O! I wish it wasn't so faint!"

Seth studied the old map again. "Maybe the three large letters in the middle go together!" he suggested.

Jed stared at him. "What do you mean?" he asked.

Seth pointed at the letters, one at a time. "Look!" he said. "O,M,C! Or, D,M,C!" He shook his head. "Whichever! I can't tell if that's supposed to be a D or an O!"

"DMC, OMC," Jed said. "What does that stand for?"

Seth shrugged. "I don't know. But I bet the letters go together!"

Suddenly, Nathan slapped the ground in excitement. "I

know what it is!" he shouted. The other two boys turned and looked at him. "Look!" he shouted. "It's DMC!"

"So what does that stand for?" Jed asked again.

"DMC!" Nathan shouted again. "Dead Man's Canyon!"

The others looked at each other, then broke into huge grins. "Nathan, you're a genius!" Jed exclaimed. "I think you're right!"

"I knew it all along," Nathan boasted.

"You knew that this was supposed to be Dead Man's Canyon?"

"No," Nathan answered, "I knew that I was a genius!"

Jed pointed at the map. "This end is the entrance to the canyon," he said, "and this end has the waterfall. This X marks the place where the gold mine is, so it's somewhere close to the end with the waterfall." He looked up at his companions. "Let's head for Dead Man's Canyon and have a look!"

"Don't be too disappointed if we don't find the mine!" Nathan warned.

"Well, we may not find it in five minutes," Jed said, "but we will find it! I know it!"

Jed carefully rolled the brittle leather map into the shape of a tube and inserted it into the rusty iron pipe. He hid it inside his shirt again. He called Wolf, and they remounted and headed for Dead Man's Canyon. Seth doubled with Nathan this time.

As the riders entered Dead Man's Canyon half an hour later, Jed was thrilled again by the rugged beauty of the canyon. "I wonder why it's called 'Dead Man's Canyon,' " he remarked.

"I hope we never find out!" Seth replied.

They rode along the edge of the stream as it flowed through the bottom of the canyon. When they passed through the narrow cleft near the waterfall, Jed dismounted and spread the map on the sand of the canyon floor. Seth and Nathan crowded in close.

"The X shows the gold mine along this edge of the canyon," Jed pointed out. "So the entrance to the mine must be along this canyon wall."

"Yeah, but where?" Nathan asked. "This canyon must be a mile and a half long! We could search for years!"

Seth pointed to the map. "See that funny-looking mountain?" he asked. "See how it looks almost like a face, with two eyes and a mouth? Those holes must be caves!" He pointed across the canyon. "Look at that cliff over there! There's the face!"

The brothers both turned and looked in the direction that Seth pointed. Sure enough, there was the "face," almost exactly as it was drawn on the map. Two small caves side by side resembled eyes, and a larger cave centered below the two "eyes" suggested a mouth.

"Well, at least we know for sure that this is the right canyon," Nathan said after studying the caves. "There's no doubt at all that those are the caves that Potter drew on his map."

"According to the map, the mine is across the canyon from the 'face,' " Jed pointed out, "and closer to the waterfall. So that means that it has to be on this side of the canyon, and farther down. Let's look over there."

The boys tied their horses in the shade and started searching the canyon on foot. "What will a gold mine look like?" Nathan asked.

"I don't know," Jed replied. "We'll start looking in some of the caves. Let's walk down closer to the waterfall, where it shows the X on the map."

"There's a cave there," Seth called, pointing at the rock

face of the canyon wall. "That's about where it shows the X on the map! Let's look there!"

Jed agreed. "I think you're right," he said. "That looks to be about the spot where the X is on Old Man Potter's map."

The trio hiked over and stood below the cave. The cave entrance was straight above them, some twenty feet up the sheer rock wall. Nathan tipped his head back and looked up at the cave, shielding his eyes from the bright afternoon sun. "How do we get up there?" he wondered aloud. "The canyon wall goes straight up!"

Seth pointed. "We could climb up that crevice there," he suggested. "Once we're up beside the cave, I think we could cross over on those tree roots hanging down. It won't be easy, but I think we can do it."

"I'll climb up!" Jed volunteered. "If I find something, you guys can come up, too. If there's nothing there, why should all three of us go?"

Seth nodded. "You're right! Go for it!"

Jed slowly worked his way up the face of the canyon wall, following the crevice to utilize the shallow handholds and footholds it afforded. His knees trembled as he climbed.

Nathan watched anxiously from below. "Careful, Jed!" he called. "If you fall from there, you'll break your neck!"

"You're right beside the tree roots now!" Seth called to him. "If you reach straight out to your left, you'll feel them. They're about three feet from you."

Jed inched carefully to his left and reached out as far as he dared. "Just a little more!" Nathan encouraged him. "Your fingers are about six inches from it!"

Cautiously, Jed leaned out farther, stretching as far as he could. His groping fingers found a thick root, and he gripped it tightly. Inch by inch, he worked his way around the face of the rock until he had a grip on the tree roots with both hands. "This isn't gonna be much fun coming back!" he called to his companions.

He scrambled across the roots, and a moment or two later, he had reached the cave. "What's in it?" Nathan called up.

Jed's voice floated down to them, echoing back from across the canyon. "You ought to see it!" he shouted. "There's gold piled all over the place! There must be two hundred pounds of gold here!"

Seth's eyes lit up at Jed's answer, and Nathan laughed. "You don't know him very well yet," he said. "He's just teasing us!"

Nathan hollered up to Jed. "Then throw some nuggets down! Part of the gold is ours too, you know!"

Jed's laugh echoed across the canyon. "Come up and get yours!" he yelled.

While the others watched breathlessly, Jed began the dangerous descent from the cave. He worked his way down the tree roots and over to the crevice. As he started down the crevice, Nathan let out his breath in a long sigh. "He's got it now!" he said to Seth.

When Jed was safely on the ground again, he turned to the others. "Well, that wasn't it," he said, "so let's check the other caves. Let me see the map again."

The boys spent the rest of the afternoon searching the canyon, but found nothing that they thought even resembled a gold mine. They crawled into every cave they came to, checked carefully along the canyon walls, even looked under trees and bushes. But they could find no trace of the legendary Bluebird Gold Mine. The sun was setting over the western rim of Dead Man's Canyon as Seth turned to the two brothers.

"Look how late it's getting!" he said in alarm. "I should

have been home an hour ago! Pa's gonna skin me alive!"

The boys hurried back to the horses and rode quickly out of the canyon. They rode to the Olson house, and Seth scrambled from the saddle. "See you fellows tomorrow!" he called as he dashed into the house. "I hope I get to go tomorrow!"

The Cartwright boys rode out to the Double-L. Nathan hid the map under the hay while Jed tended to the horses. "I put it in the same place you did," he told Jed as he climbed down from the loft. "I can't wait till we can search that canyon again tomorrow!"

Mrs. Laramy met Jed and Nathan at the kitchen door. "Supper's over," she told them. "We ate without you. Yours is sitting on the dining room table. Next time, please try to let me know if you are going to be late."

"Sorry, Mrs. Laramy," Jed said meekly as they entered the kitchen. "We didn't realize how late it was getting."

"I'm not upset with you," the gentle woman said. "I know how times flies when you're having fun with your friends. Just try to let me know ahead of time."

The next morning seemed like it was a hundred years long. The schoolwork dragged on and on. The boys could hardly sit still, thinking about Dead Man's Canyon and the lost gold mine out there, just waiting for them to find it. Finally, lunch was over and the boys headed for the barn.

"You saddle up," Jed suggested. "I'll get the map." He climbed the ladder to the loft.

Nathan was saddling the second horse when Jed called down, "Hey, Nate! What did you do with the map?"

"It's in the same place." Nathan answered. "It's under the hay, right where you put it before."

"I can't find it!" Jed called.

"I'll be right up," Nathan replied. He cinched the saddle girth tightly, then led the horse over to the door and threw the reins over a rail. He climbed the ladder to the loft. "It's right over here!" he said as he walked through the hay. "I put it under the edge of this bale, like you did."

He lifted the edge of the bale, then began to dig furiously in the hay beneath it. Finally, he looked at Jed in alarm. The rusty iron pipe was nowhere to be found. Their valuable map was gone!

The boys climbed back down the ladder. "Are you sure you put it there?" Jed questioned.

Nathan looked crestfallen. "I know I did, Jed!" he insisted. "I'm positive! I put it right under the edge of that bale, exactly where you put it before!"

"Hey, Nate, look!" Jed exclaimed. He picked up a pouch of tobacco from the dusty barn floor. "Where did this come from?"

Nathan shook his head. "Somebody was in the barn last night!" he said, wide-eyed. "Mr. Laramy doesn't chew, and neither do any of the ranch hands."

The boys looked at each other. "Someone came in here last night and stole the map!" Jed whispered. "How did anyone even know it was here?"

They told Seth about it when they reached his house. "I'm afraid the map is gone forever!" Nathan finished sadly. "Whoever stole it is not going to bring it back!"

"What do we do now?" Seth asked.

"We go out to the canyon and find the mine anyway!" Jed said fiercely. "We all studied the map quite a bit. I think I could draw it from memory! But we have to find the mine fast, before the thief finds it!"

The boys rode to Dead Man's Canyon. Like they had done

the day before, they tied their horses in the shade and prepared to search for the mine on foot. Jed picked up a stick and started drawing in the sand.

"Here's what the map looked like," he said. "You tell me if you think I have all the details right." He drew the canyon, the creek, and all the mountains and caves as he remembered them. "What do you think?" he asked when he had finished.

The others agreed that Jed's version of the map was accurate. Nathan took a stick and wrote "D, M, C" down the center of Jed's canyon.

"Why did you make the M that way?" Seth asked. "What's the little tail for?"

"That's the way it looked on Potter's map," Nathan answered. He looked at Jed. "Didn't it?"

Jed nodded. "You're right. It was a funny-looking M."

"Let's go to the area marked with the X again," Seth suggested. "Maybe we missed something yesterday!"

"Maybe there was a cave-in twenty or twenty-five years ago, and the entrance to the mine isn't there any longer!" Jed suggested dismally.

The boys searched the canyon walls just as they had done the day before, but again without success. "I don't think there is a gold mine in this canyon!" Nathan remarked disgustedly.

"Look! Someone's coming!" Seth whispered, pointing. The others whirled around. A man in a red flannel shirt was walking into the canyon. He looked from side to side continually as if he was watching for someone.

"Hide!" Jed hissed urgently. "We don't want him to know that we're here!" He ran back to where the map was drawn in the sand and rubbed it out with his boot.

As the boy dashed to where the others crouched behind a clump of prickly pear cactus, a rifle shot echoed in the canyon, and a bullet ricocheted off the rock wall over the boys' heads. Jed dived in beside the others. The rifle cracked again, and a second bullet whined past them. "He's shooting at us!" Jed cried in disbelief.

A third shot echoed across the canyon, and again the boys heard the whine of the bullet. "Look!" Nathan cried out. "That one was close!"

Jed and Seth gasped as they saw where Nathan was pointing. A large chunk had been shot out of one of the "ears" of the prickly pear cactus in front of them, and the juice of the plant was spattered all over Nathan's shirt.

"He's not just trying to scare us!" Seth cried in alarm. "He's trying to kill us! We've got to get out of here!"

Danger in the Canyon

The man in the red shirt came closer. He walked slowly, deliberately, as if he knew that his intended prey was cornered and without possible escape. "We've got to get out of here!" Seth said again. "He saw us!"

"Maybe we could hide behind the waterfall!" Nathan suggested.

Jed began crawling back away from the cactus they were hiding behind. "Let's see if we can make it to the canyon wall," he told the others. "We can't stay here!"

The man raised the rifle to his shoulder, and Seth called, "Get down!" A shot ricocheted off the rocks behind them.

Seth and Nathan crawled after Jed. "We're trapped!" Seth whispered. "He's got us boxed in! The canyon is a dead end!"

"Keep crawling!" Jed urged. "If we can make it behind that rocky ridge over there, he can't see us! Maybe we can hide in a cave until we can figure a way to get out of here!" The man in the red shirt fired two more shots, but the boys made it to the rocky ridge safely. Nathan peered out from behind a rock.

"What's he doing now?" Seth asked.

"He's just standing there," Nathan answered. "It looks like he's reloading his rifle."

"Maybe we can rush him!" Seth suggested.

Nathan shook his head. "He's still a hundred yards away!" he said. "We'd never get to him in time!"

"I wish we had our rifles!" Jed muttered. "I could outshoot this guy, any day!"

Nathan nodded, and looked at Seth. "Jed's good with a rifle!" he agreed.

"I have an idea!" Jed suddenly whispered. "Quick, Nate! Give me your hat and shirt!" He began to peel off his own shirt as he said this.

Nathan looked at his brother with a puzzled expression, then took off his shirt and hat without questioning what Jed had in mind. "See that thick clump of sage brush?" Jed pointed as he snatched the hat and shirt from Nathan. "Our man can't see us right now. You guys crawl under the brush and lay flat! I'll be right back. But hurry!"

Crouching low, Jed ran along the backside of the ridge and disappeared from view. He peered around the end of the ridge just in time to see Seth and Nathan scrambling under a thick clump of sagebrush. Quietly, Jed returned to some bushes near where the others were waiting.

"What's Jed doing?" Jed heard Seth whisper.

"I don't know, but he's up to something!" Nathan replied. "I've seen that look in his eyes before!"

"I just hope it works!" Seth said. "If not, then we're dead ducks!"

"Lie still!" Jed warned in a whisper. "He's coming!"

The boys pressed their bodies flat against the rocky ground, hardly daring to breathe. Their attacker strode into view. He was tall and broad-shouldered, and more than a little overweight. His red shirt sagged and bulged. The man carried the rifle in front of him, and swung his head from side to side as he searched for the boys. His hat was pulled low over his eyes, so the boys could not see his face.

The man passed within thirty feet of the boys' hiding place. Three trembling boys, faces white with fear, silently asked God to keep the man from seeing them. The man walked by the clump of brush without spotting them and then paused just a few paces beyond them. He turned, his eyes scanning the canyon.

Jed picked up a large rock. "When I say go, be ready to scramble out of here and get to the other side of the ridge again," he whispered. "We've got to move quick, and we've got to be quiet!"

The man walked a few steps farther down the canyon, and Jed quietly raised up from behind the bushes. "Get ready!" he whispered. He hurled the rock as far as he could, behind and beyond the man with the rifle. When the rock struck the side of a large boulder, the man instantly whirled toward the sound. He began walking over to investigate with his gun ready.

"Let's go!" Jed whispered. The three frightened boys slid noiselessly from their hiding place. Crouching low, they scrambled around the end of the ridge. A moment later, the boys heard several gunshots.

In spite of his fear, Jed snickered. "He's shooting at our shirts!" he told the others softly as they ran. The boys ran until they had slipped through the narrow passage in the canyon. On the other side of the cleft, Jed stopped to catch his breath. Two more shots rang out.

"He can't see us now!" Jed said, breathing hard. "Let's head for the horses! I think we're gonna make it!"

The boys ran again, not stopping until they had reached the horses. "I was afraid he might have let the horses loose!" Seth said as Jed and Nathan scrambled into the saddles. He quickly climbed up behind Jed, and the boys rode breathlessly out of the canyon.

When they were safely away from Dead Man's Canyon, Nathan turned to face Jed. "What did you do with our hats and shirts?" he asked.

Jed laughed. "I just tried an old trick that Pa showed me," he answered. "I hung the shirts on the side of a bush, and placed the hats on top of the bush. When I threw the rock, I tried to land it close to the bush, so he would see the shirts and think it was us. Apparently, it worked. I knew it would only fool him for a few seconds, but I figured that was all we needed!"

The boys stopped their mounts at the edge of town. "What do you think?" Jed asked the others. "Do we go back tomorrow? It could be dangerous again!"

Seth nodded. "I say we go back," he voted. "We've got to find that gold mine! We're gonna lose our house in just a few more days!"

Nathan nodded also. "I say we go back, too!"

Jed grinned. "Good!" he said. "Then it's settled! We go back tomorrow! I want to find the Bluebird Mine and help Pastor Wood with his church!" He suddenly gritted his teeth. "But tomorrow, Nate, we take our rifles! And, Wolf is going along! If that man comes back, he'll have a battle on his hands!"

The boys rode to the Olsons' barn and sat in the hay, discussing the attack. "I think it's the guy that stole the map!" Nathan said. "I saw him spit tobacco juice when he was reloading."

"I don't think we should tell anyone about this right now," Jed suggested. "Mr. and Mrs. Laramy won't let us go to the canyon if they know about it, and your Pa probably won't either! But, we've got to find the mine before that man does!"

"If Aunt Lou or Ma knew about it," Seth said, "they'd use it as an excuse to keep me home helping them with the chores! Let's not tell anyone yet!"

Jed stood up and led his horse from the barn. "Well, Nate, we'd better head home," he said. The next minute, he was lying on the ground beside a rusty old plow. The goat had struck again!

Nathan laughed as he swung into his saddle. "You weren't watching!" he snickered. "See you tomorrow!" he called to Seth as they rode from the yard.

The boys rode down Main Street, heading toward the Double-L. Suddenly, Jed drew his horse to a stop. "Look!" he said, pointing. Nathan looked over in time to see the man with the red shirt disappear into the bank. Their attacker was in town!

The Hidden Canyon

Jed led his mount across the street and tied up in front of an implement store. "Let's watch to see who he is when he comes out!" he said to Nathan.

The boys ran across the street toward the bank. Jed stopped and crouched behind a hogshead barrel on the boardwalk. Nathan joined him. "We can see his face from here when he comes out," Jed whispered. "Maybe we can find out who he is."

The door opened suddenly, and the boys ducked lower behind the hogshead. But the customer coming out of the bank was a woman in a black satin dress. Nathan let out his breath slowly.

Several minutes passed. The door opened again, and the boys crouched lower. "It's him!" Jed whispered.

The man in the red shirt passed just a few feet from their hiding place. Jed sighed. This wasn't their attacker after all! This man was thin, and his chest was nearly covered by a long, gray beard.

The Cartwrights walked back to their horses. "If that was the man in the canyon," Jed laughed, "he has sure lost weight."

"And grew that beard mighty fast!" Nathan added.

The next day was Saturday, and the boys helped Mr. Laramy with some morning chores around the ranch. "You've done enough, boys," the tall man finally said. "Why don't you take the rest of the day off?"

"You saddle the horses," Jed called to Nathan. "I'll get the guns." He headed for the ranch house as his brother entered the barn.

"I can go all day!" Seth told them excitedly when they reached his house. "Aunt Lou is off visiting some friends for several days, and Ma said that I deserve some time off, too!" He climbed up behind Nathan, then spotted the rifles. "Are they loaded?" he asked.

Jed shook his head. "We'll stop and load before we reach Dead Man's Canyon, though."

Twenty minutes later, they rode cautiously into the canyon. "I think we ought to hide the horses," Jed said, "just in case our attacker comes back. We can put them in the entrance to that big cave on the south wall."

The boys rode slowly through the canyon, eyes searching for the man in the red flannel shirt. The Cartwrights both cocked their rifles and held the weapons at the ready. They reached the cave without seeing any sign of the man and tied their mounts behind the trees at the entrance.

Wolf disappeared into the brush, but Jed called him back. "Stay close, boy!" he ordered.

"I can't believe how well that dog obeys you!" Seth marveled.

Jed laughed. "He knows who's boss!" He ruffled the big dog's fur. "Don't you, boy?"

The boys and the dog searched the canyon again. Two hours went by, but they found nothing. They searched and researched the area indicated by the X on Old Man Potter's map, but found the search was fruitless.

"Let's break for lunch," Jed finally suggested. "I'm starving!"

The boys walked back to the horses and Nathan opened the saddlebags. He took the lunch that Mrs. Laramy had prepared for them, and passed some of it to the others. All three boys sat on top of a huge boulder enjoying the delicious lunch and cool water from the canteen. Jed had his pocketknife out, carving a piece of cholla wood as he ate. The loaded rifles were propped against the base of the rock.

Suddenly, Jed closed the knife and jumped from the big rock. The other boys dropped their sandwiches and scrambled down in alarm. Nathan reached for his rifle. "What is it, Jed?" Seth asked. "Is someone coming?"

Jed shook his head. "I just want to draw the map again," he answered. "We've searched this whole section of the canyon, but the mine's not here! Maybe we're overlooking something!"

He broke a stick from a mesquite and drew in the sand. The others watched him. "There!" he said, when the map was finished. "Did I leave out anything?"

Nathan took the stick and wrote "D,M,C" down the center of Jed's canyon. He took great care to make the curly tail on the letter M, just as it had been on the map.

The boys knelt in the sand and studied Jed's map. "This is the way I remember Old Man Potter's map," Jed said. "I don't think I left anything out!" He pointed to the X in the sand. "This is where we are right now, across the canyon from the 'face.' We've searched this whole area! So, where is the gold mine?"

The boys studied the sand map in silence. Finally, Seth

spoke. "Why do you always make that funny tail on the letter M?" he asked. "You did that last time, too!"

"That's the way it was on Old Man's Potter's leather map," Nathan explained. "So I just drew it the same way!"

Jed leaned forward intently. "Is that exactly the way it was drawn?" he asked eagerly.

Nathan looked at Jed in surprise. "I think so," he replied. He studied the sand drawing again, then wiped out the letter M. "Actually," he said, "I think the letter was down farther, more to the side of the canyon. I noticed that on Potter's map it wasn't in a straight line with the D and the C." He picked up the stick and rewrote the M again complete with curly tail. The letter was closer to the wall of the canyon.

Jed looked at the others. "I think Old Man Potter played a little trick when he drew the map," he said mysteriously.

"You mean you don't think there really is a gold mine?" Seth asked in disappointment.

Jed shook his head. "No, I don't mean that," he replied. "But I think maybe he drew the X in the wrong place on the map! On purpose!"

The others stared at him. "Then, how are you supposed to find the right place?" Nathan asked.

Jed pointed to the drawing in the sand. "Have you ever wondered," he questioned, "why Potter drew the M so strangely? It's so different from the D and the C."

He pointed to the little tail on the M. "Look at the way the line crosses itself!" he said. He reached out and drew a small square around the tail. "What do you see?" he asked. "Just inside the square!"

The others stared at Jed's drawing. "It's an X!" Seth said in astonishment.

"Right!" Jed replied. "When the tail of the M crosses itself, it forms a small X! Maybe this X marks the spot for the Bluebird Mine, and the other X was just to throw people off the trail."

The others thought it over. "Could be!" Seth said finally. He looked again at the map in the sand. "If that's true," he said, "then we've been hunting in the wrong part of the canyon! We need to go back through the pass and search in the wide part of the canyon!"

"Exactly!" Jed agreed. "At least, it's worth a try!" The boys rubbed out the map, picked up the two rifles, and untied their horses. Wolf sprang to his feet, sensing their excitement. The boys rode through the pass, then paused on the other side to survey the canyon. They sat silently for several minutes carefully scanning the canyon for any sign of their visitor of the day before.

"Let's tie the horses in the shade over there," Jed suggested. "That way, they'll be out of sight in case anyone comes into the canyon."

When the horses were tied, Seth and Nathan followed Jed across to the north side of the canyon. "If the tail of the M marks the location of the mine, then it should be right around here," Jed said, assessing their position in the canyon. "Let's search along the canyon wall."

The boys searched for hours, checking every cave, examining nearly every foot of the canyon wall, but finding nothing. Finally, Seth glanced up at the sun. "What time is it getting to be?" he asked.

Nathan pulled out his watch and looked at it. "Four- thirty," he said.

"We need to leave in half an hour, okay?" Seth asked. "I've gotta be home on time tonight."

Jed sat down beside a small trickling stream and sketched

the map again in the dirt. "Maybe the M doesn't mark the location of the mine," he said. "We've searched this whole area!"

Nathan looked at the map on the ground. "Did Potter's map show this little creek?" he asked.

Jed shook his head. "I don't think so," he replied. "It showed the main creek, the one that this flows into. But I don't think it showed this one. The M on the map is about where this creek would be."

All three boys looked at each other, then jumped to their feet. "Let's follow the creek up!" Seth shouted excitedly. "Let's see where it comes out of the canyon wall!"

The boys traced the little stream until they came to a dense thicket. The thicket grew against the canyon wall, concealing the source of the stream.

"If the Bluebird Mine is in there, it's no wonder that no one has ever found it!" Nathan commented. "You'd never see it, even if you were looking for it!"

The boys began to push their way through the thick brambles. They finally got on their knees and crawled most of the way in. Jed was in the lead, and as he crawled out of the thicket he suddenly realized that they were in another small canyon, a section that was not visible from the main one. Seth and Nathan crawled out of the brambles after him.

"Look at this, guys!" Jed said excitedly. "We're in a separate section of the canyon! That rock ledge keeps you from seeing this canyon, unless you go through the brambles!"

The hidden canyon was small, perhaps fifteen or twenty feet wide and a hundred feet long. The little stream flowed through the center of it. At the upper end of the canyon, the stream bubbled out of a dark opening in the rocks.

Jed pointed to the cave. "Gentlemen," he said dramatically, "welcome to the legendary Bluebird Gold Mine!"

The three boys raced for the dark hole in the side of the mountain with Wolf close behind. Jed set his rifle down and crawled into the opening. The cave was unusually cool. "Come on in!" he called to the others. "There's nothing to be afraid of!"

Wolf followed Seth and Nathan into the dark passage. The boys crawled back into the side of the hill until they could no longer see. "We need to get some lanterns," Seth said. "I can't see a thing!"

As the boys crawled back toward daylight, Jed saw Wolf nosing around behind a large rock. He went over to the dog. "What did you find, boy?" Suddenly his eyes widened, and he picked up two objects from the ground. Jed hurried to catch up with the others. "Look what I found, fellows!" he called as he stepped out into the bright sunshine.

His two companions turned around. "Where did you get those?"

"They were in the cave!" Jed answered, holding up a miner's pick and a rusty coal oil lantern. "Wolf found them!"

The three boys examined the old pick and lantern. "This must be the mine!" Seth exulted. "We found it!" He turned the lantern over. On the bottom, barely visible, two initials were scratched into the metal. The letters were—JP!

"This is Old Man Potter's lantern!" Nathan said excitedly. "Let's get some lanterns and come back tomorrow! I bet there's tons of gold, just waiting for us to find it!"

Jed shook his head. "Tomorrow's Sunday," he reminded his brother. "We promised Pastor Wood that we would come to church."

"But what if the man with the red shirt comes and finds the mine before we get back?" Nathan argued. "He'll claim all the gold!"

"We'll just have to wait until Monday!" Jed insisted. "You
know that church is more important than anything else, even
a gold mine!"

The boys picked up their rifles and walked back down the
small canyon. Seth was carrying Old Man Potter's pick and
lantern. "Remember, not a word about this to anyone!" Jed
said as they bent down to crawl through the bramble thicket.

Jed, who was in the lead, emerged from the thicket, and
Wolf gave a low growl. Jed shrank back into the brambles
immediately, laying a hand on Wolf's neck to quiet him. He
then saw the cause of Wolf's agitation.

The man in the red shirt was riding through the canyon
on an old mule with a rifle resting across the saddle in front
of him. He turned from side to side, scanning the canyon as
he rode. His right hand was on the reins, and in his left hand
he carried a short length of rusty iron pipe.

The man's hat was pulled low over his eyes, and again
Jed could not see his face. Jed quietly levered a bullet into the
chamber of his rifle. *We have a fighting chance this time!* he
told himself.

Seth crawled up beside Jed, silently watching the man as
he rode by. The intruder passed within fifty yards of the boys.
"I know that man from somewhere," Seth whispered to the
others when the rider was safely out of earshot. "I couldn't
see his face, but there was something familiar about him. I
know him from somewhere!"

"He had the map!" Nathan whispered fiercely. "I knew it!
He's the one that broke into the barn!"

Jed nodded grimly as he watched the man ride down the
canyon. "We've got to come back and find the gold before he
does!" he said. "We've just got to!"

The Bluebird Gold Mine

Sunday morning, Jed woke Nathan, and they both dressed quickly. "We'll have to get our own breakfast," Jed told his brother. "I think Mrs. Laramy is still in bed."

But when the boys reached the kitchen, their hostess was already there, dressed in a tattered housecoat. Bacon was frying on the stove. She laughed as the boys entered the room. "Nathan," she said, "it looks like you had a rough night! I think you should have stayed in bed!"

The boy shook his head, rubbing the sleep from his eyes. "I couldn't," he explained. "Jed and I are going to church this morning."

The woman looked surprised. "We don't have a church in Hard Luck," she said.

"Yes, there is!" Nathan insisted. "Pastor Wood invited us!"

"Is that the man that has meetings in his house?" Mrs. Laramy asked. When the boys nodded, she scoffed, "That's not a real church! Imagine! Holding church in a house! That's not a proper way to worship, and that man has no right calling it a church!"

The boys ate breakfast, then walked into town. "I see what Pastor Wood means about people not coming because they don't have a real church building," Jed said to Nathan as they strolled along in their Sunday clothes. "Even Mrs. Laramy feels that way! I hope we find the gold soon so he can build a regular church building."

"How much does a church cost?" Nathan asked.

"I don't know," Jed answered, "but Pa would, since he paid for the church in St. Louis."

Pastor Wood greeted the boys warmly at the door of his "church" house. "Good to see you, boys!" he said. "I'm glad you could make it!"

He led the boys into the house and introduced them to his wife. Mrs. Wood was a friendly woman with long, dark hair. She held a small baby on her lap. "It's good to meet you, Jed and Nathan," she smiled. "You're just in time! We're about ready to start."

The boys looked around the room in surprise. Besides Mr. and Mrs. Wood, there were only three other adults and four children. "I thought there would be more people," Jed whispered to Nathan.

But the service was like a service in a regular church. Pastor Wood led the "congregation" in hymn singing, then stood before them and preached a Gospel message. He gave an invitation at the close of the service, but no one went forward.

The friendly pastor shook their hands at the door. "Glad to have you, boys!" he said again. "I hope you can come next week."

Both boys nodded. "I think we can," Nathan told him. As they walked toward the Double-L, Nathan said, "We need to invite Seth next week. I think he would come, and he needs to hear the Gospel!" Jed nodded his agreement.

Monday morning, the boys found it almost impossible to keep their minds on their studies. The Bluebird Gold Mine was waiting! But both boys did their best to pay attention as Mr. Phelps gave them assignments. Finally, the long morning was over.

The boys hurried into the kitchen and asked Mrs. Laramy if they could pack a lunch. The kind lady was happy to oblige them, and in just a few minutes, they were ready to head out. Jed had filled an extra canteen.

While they were saddling up, Nathan pulled some money from his pocket. "We'll need to get lanterns in town," he told Jed.

His brother nodded. "Good thinking!" he said approvingly. "Why don't I stop in at the general store and get three of them while you take the rifles and pick up Seth."

When they reached the store, Nathan waved to Jed. "We'll meet you right here in front," he called.

Jed found three lanterns in the store and took them up to the counter. The clerk was a cross-looking man with curly blond hair and a thin mustache. He looked at Jed suspiciously. "What do you need three lanterns for, Son?" he asked.

Jed knew that he dared not mention the gold mine. He thought quickly. "It got mighty dark last night!" he said with a nervous laugh. He laid his money on the counter.

The man filled the lanterns from a metal container and then set a box of matches beside them. "I'll throw the matches in free," he said.

"Could I get some more oil?" Jed asked.

The man frowned and set the container on the counter. "That will be an extra dollar," he said. "I don't see how you'll use that much oil!"

Jed paid for his purchases, and then tried to carry the three lanterns and the can of coal oil.

"Wait!" the clerk said. He pulled a gunnysack from under the counter and carefully placed the three lanterns in it. He handed the sack to Jed. "Here. But be careful!"

When Jed walked out of the store, Seth and Nathan were waiting on the horses. Jed handed the gunnysack up to Seth, who then looped it over the saddle horn. Holding the can of coal oil, Jed climbed up behind Nathan, and they were off for Dead Man's Canyon.

"Do you think we'll see 'you-know-who'?" Seth asked as they neared the canyon.

"I hope not," Jed answered, "but we'll be ready!" He stopped and loaded both rifles carefully, then handed one to Seth, who put it back in the saddle scabbard.

A wave of excitement swept over the boys as they rode into the canyon. Today was the day when they were actually going to enter the mine! The trio hid the horses, then hiked across the canyon to the bramble thicket. They kept a sharp eye out for the man in the red shirt, but he did not make an appearance. They crawled painfully through the thick brambles and then stood staring at the entrance to the Bluebird Gold Mine.

Jed pulled the lanterns from the sack. "Now to see if these things will light!" he said. He adjusted the wick in the first lamp, lit a match, and held it to the wick. After a moment, the lantern burned steadily.

When all three lanterns were lit, the boys crawled into the darkness of the mine tunnel. "It gives you a creepy feeling, doesn't it?" Seth called, and his voice echoed in the dark chamber ahead.

They entered a long tunnel. The ceiling was easily high

enough for them to stand up, and they gratefully got to their feet.

"Look at this!" Jed whistled softly. "Old Man Potter must have spent years working in here!"

The mine tunnel, several feet wide, stretched ahead as far as the boys could see in the feeble light from their lanterns. The little stream flowed through the center of the tunnel. Heavy timbers nearly a foot square shored up the roof of the tunnel every few feet. As they walked along, they passed other shafts leading off in different directions.

"Maybe he had other people working with him," Nathan suggested.

Suddenly, Jed stopped. "Where's Wolf?" he said. "I forgot all about him!"

"He was with us when we crawled through the brambles," Seth said. "But I don't think he came with us into the mine."

The boys hurried back to the mine entrance. Jed called for Wolf, but got no response. "Stay here; I'll be right back!" he told his companions as he hurried toward the entrance to the hidden canyon. Jed crawled out into the main section of Dead Man's Canyon, but there was no sign of his dog. He called several times, then made his way back into the hidden canyon.

"I can't find him," he told Seth and Nathan, "but he'll show up! He'll find us again when we come back out of the mine."

The boys crawled back into the cavern. "Look at this!" Jed called. The others hurried over to him. Jed pointed. "That wasn't here Saturday!" Embedded in the soft earth of the cave floor was a large print of a man's boot.

Jed placed his own boot beside the print. "It's even bigger than mine," he said, "so it wasn't made by one of us! Someone else has found the mine!"

Seth held his lantern high. "And look at this!" he said. "I know this can't be thirty years old!"

Lying on the floor was a large, black, wet wad of chewing tobacco. The boys looked at each other. "The man in the red shirt!" Nathan said.

"What if he's in here now?" Seth asked, his voice quavering just a little.

Jed shook his head. "I don't think he is!" he decided. "And even if he is, we have two rifles!"

The boys resumed their trip into the dark gold mine, but their hearts beat a little faster. A pebble fell from the ceiling, and all three jumped in fright at the sound. "I think we should stay in the main tunnel for now," Jed suggested as they walked along. "We could get lost if we start following every little side tunnel. We'll need to mark a trail carefully when we go into them."

A few minutes later, the boys stopped at the edge of a huge underground room. The room was nearly a hundred feet long and just about as wide, and the ceiling was some thirty feet above their heads.

"Old Man Potter didn't dig this!" Seth declared. "This is a natural cavern!"

The boys walked into the vast chamber and stood staring at the beauty of the place. Large white stalactites hung from the ceiling, and magnificent rock formations decorated the walls and floor. The walls of the cavern glittered and sparkled as though they were encrusted with a million jewels, even in the dim light of the lanterns.

"It's an underground palace!" Seth exclaimed.

Jed, Nathan, and Seth stood staring at the underground splendor. Finally, almost reverently, they walked through the huge cavern, silently drinking in the beauty that surrounded them.

Little soda straw stalactites hung in clusters from the ceiling, and beautiful crystalline cave flowers graced some of the walls. The little stream flowed through the center of the beautiful room.

Jed spotted a pile of timbers stacked against one wall of the cavern and carried his lantern over to investigate. He climbed up the pile of wood and waved his lantern to attract the attention of Seth and Nathan. "Hey, fellows, I'm over here!" he called.

Just then, the timber beneath Jed's feet shifted, and the whole stack came tumbling down. Jed fell backwards, and his head struck the rock wall of the cavern. He saw a bright flash of light, then suddenly, everything was darkness.

When Jed came to, Seth and Nathan were standing over him with worried looks on their faces. He turned his head to one side, groaning in pain. The lantern lay beside him, its glass chimney shattered in a thousand pieces. A dark puddle of coal oil was slowly spreading across the cavern floor. Seth picked up the lantern and set it upright on a large rock.

"Is he all right?" Nathan asked anxiously.

Jed closed his eyes, then opened them again. He stared up into the frightened faces of Nathan and Seth. "What happened?" he asked weakly.

Nathan grinned broadly. "You're gonna be all right!" he said happily.

"What?" Jed sat up, holding the back of his head gingerly.

"You knocked this pile of wood over, and I guess you hit your head against the wall," Nathan replied. "But it looks like you're gonna be all right."

Seth and Nathan helped Jed to his feet. "My head feels like it was kicked by a mule," he said, "but I guess I'll live." He turned and looked at the pile of timbers that he had knocked down. Suddenly, his eyes lit up. "Hey, look at this!"

The rounded edge of a dull metal object was now visible beneath the end of one of the timbers. Jed pointed to it. "Do you know what that is?" he asked excitedly. Without waiting for a reply, he answered his own question. "It's one of those pans they use for panning gold!"

The boys began to remove the remaining timbers. The beams were heavy, but the three of them were able to drag them one by one. "Maybe Old Man Potter didn't dig that much gold ore from this mine," Jed said. "Maybe he panned nuggets out of the stream!"

After a lot of grunting and groaning, the boys removed the last of the heavy timbers and the bottom of the pan was completely exposed. The boys could now see that it was upside down.

Jed reached down and tried to lift the pan. The edge was buried in the dirt, and the object wouldn't budge. He pulled his knife from his pocket and dug furiously at the dirt. Finally, the pan was free.

Jed folded the knife closed and put it back in his pocket. Seth reached over and lifted the pan, and the boys stared in amazement. A large pile of shiny gold nuggets glittered in the feeble light from the lanterns!

Cave-In

The three boys were awestruck. For a full minute they knelt silently, gazing at the glittering, golden pile of precious metal before them. "My word!" Seth exclaimed at last. "There must be hundreds of dollars in gold here!"

Jed laughed happily. "More like thousands!" he corrected. "I've never seen this much money in all my life!"

Nathan reached out and grabbed a fistful of the nuggets. "They're heavy!" he uttered in surprise.

Jed nodded. "It's real gold, all right!"

The boys ran their fingers through the pile of gold, and then began to fill their pockets with the glittering nuggets. Their pockets bulged with the heavy metal. Jed pulled the gunnysack from his belt. "Here," he said, "I forgot this! We can fill it with the rest of the gold!"

The excited boys scooped the nuggets into the sack. They discovered that there was more than just the pile on top of the ground; a shallow hole had been dug and the gold filled the hole. When the nuggets were all in the sack, it was nearly one-third full.

Jed closed the mouth of the gunnysack and lifted it over

his shoulder. Or rather, he tried to lift it. To his amazement, he found that he couldn't even move the sack! "There must be two hundred pounds of gold in here!" he exclaimed as he raked nuggets back into the hole. "We'll take as much as we can carry, and come back for the rest!"

The boys dumped a good portion of the precious metal back into the ground and replaced the iron pan over it again. They strained as they scooted a heavy timber back over the pan. "That should do it!" Nathan said. "We'll come back for the rest."

The boys retraced their steps through the large cavern, Jed lugging the heavy sack over his shoulder. Seth and Nathan carried the two remaining lanterns. Seth gave a sudden war whoop and leaped into the air. "We did it!" he shouted. "We found the gold! Now we can keep the house and Pa can keep his shop!" He gave another mighty leap.

"When we get outside, don't tell the whole world about it!" Jed said dryly.

They passed from the cavern into the mine tunnel. Their footsteps echoed down the dark, empty corridor. After several minutes, Jed swung the sack of gold to the ground. "I've gotta rest!" he told the others. "This stuff is heavy!"

Seth handed him the lantern he was carrying. "I'll tote the sack a while," he offered.

Nathan suddenly held up one hand. "Listen!" he said urgently.

The three boys froze in the tunnel, listening intently. "There it is again!" Nathan whispered. And then the others heard it, too. They were standing still, but footsteps echoed down the dark corridor!

"Quick!" Jed hissed. "Get into one of the side tunnels!"

Nathan snatched one of the lanterns, and Seth grabbed

the other. Jed reached over for the gunnysack of gold. At that moment, the blast of a gunshot boomed through the corridor, and the lantern in Nathan's hand shattered! The boys raced down the corridor and dived into a mineshaft leading to the side, leaving the gold sitting in the main tunnel.

Jed stuck his head around the corner and saw a light bobbing toward them in the darkness. The gun roared again, and the frightened boy jerked his head back.

"The rifles!" Nathan groaned. "We left them in the big cavern when we found the gold!"

"It's the man with the red shirt!" Jed told the others. "I'm almost sure of it!"

"He's crazy!" Seth gritted angrily. "Those gunshots are going to make this whole place cave in!"

The gun barked again, and the boys heard the whine of the bullet as it ricocheted through the tunnel. Their hearts pounded with fear, and their faces looked a ghastly white in the feeble glow from the one remaining lantern.

"What do we do now?" Nathan whispered. "He's gonna kill us!"

"We'll have to head down this tunnel," Jed replied. "But stay together! We only have one lantern now!"

At that moment, a tremendous roar filled the entire subterranean passage. It grew louder and louder, until it seemed to the boys as though they could actually feel the sound instead of hear it. Suddenly, everything was dark, and the boys could not breathe. Dust filled the air, and they choked and coughed.

"What's happening?" Nathan cried in terror.

"It's a cave-in!" Jed yelled. "Lie down on the floor where the air is cleaner and cover your head with your hands!"

The roar increased and the dust grew thicker. For several

terrifying moments, it seemed to the frightened boys that the whole world was being destroyed. Jed lay against the wall of the tunnel, shielding his face with his arms, choking and coughing in the dust. Finally, the noise subsided, and an unearthly quiet prevailed.

The boys raised their heads. The air was still thick with dust. "Is— is everyone all right?" Jed asked.

"I'm here!" Seth answered.

"Me, too!" Nathan replied, and Jed breathed a sigh of relief.

"The light has gone out!" Seth cried out in alarm.

"No, it's not!" Nathan answered. "It's just covered in dust!"

"The noise of the gunshots must have been enough to disturb a weak place in the roof of the tunnel," Seth guessed.

The boys sat quietly, but the frightening sound of the footsteps was not repeated. Jed ventured to peer cautiously around the corner into the main corridor, but the bobbing light was gone. There was no sign of their assailant.

When the dust had subsided somewhat, the boys ventured cautiously out into the main tunnel, coughing and choking in the thick dust that still hung in the air. They walked up the tunnel, toward the cavern they had just passed through. A terrifying sight met their eyes. Ten yards or so from where they stood, the tunnel was completely blocked by huge boulders!

They cautiously approached the wall of rocks. "Look!" Jed said in horror. He pointed and held the lantern higher. The bottom of a man's boot was visible at the lower edge of the pile of boulders. Their attacker had perished in the cave-in!

The boys stared in silent horror at the gruesome sight of

the boot, then turned and hurried down the corridor. They passed the entrance to the tunnel they had taken refuge in, and a moment later stood stunned by the sight that met their eyes. The other end of the tunnel had also collapsed, blocking their only avenue of escape!

Prisoners in Darkness

Jed, Seth, and Nathan stood in the dark corridor of the gold mine, staring helplessly at the tons of rock that sealed off their only exit. Seth began to tremble so violently that the lantern shook in his hand, and Jed wordlessly took it from him.

No one said a word for several minutes. Each boy fully realized that they now faced almost certain death in the dark tunnels of the long lost gold mine. Not a soul in Hard Luck knew the location of the mine except the man who had stolen their map and attacked them, and he now lay dead under the many tons of rock that blocked the other end of the main tunnel. They had not even told anyone where they were going! And even if they had, there was no way anyone would be able to dig successfully through the cave-in! The boys knew that their doom was sealed.

Seth was the first to speak. "There's no way out!" he whispered in a voice that trembled with fear. "What are we going to do?"

"I guess the only thing to do is pray!" Jed said. "It will take a miracle for us to get out of this place!"

The trembling boys knelt in the dusty tunnel of the mine and begged God to hear and help them. They asked for wisdom as to what they should do. Seth was crying as they finished. The tears left muddy trails down his dusty cheeks.

Jed picked up their one remaining lantern and shook it gently. "I don't think we should just sit here," he said. "I think we have one or two hours' worth of oil left in the lantern. If we're going to do anything, we have to do it now!"

Nathan looked at his brother, amazed that he could be so calm in such a desperate situation. "What can we do?" he asked.

"First of all, we have to stay together, no matter what!" the boy answered. "I think we should explore the side tunnel that we were just in, and see if perhaps it leads anywhere. We also need to find something to mark a trail every step we take, so we don't end up going in circles. We may not have much hope of getting out, but we can't just sit here and wait to die!"

The boys walked back toward the side tunnel. The darkness seemed to accent their despair and gloom, and the feeble light from just one lantern did little to dispel it.

Somehow they passed the side tunnel without seeing it, and ended up facing the pile of rocks that had buried their unknown attacker. "Look!" Nathan cried. His lantern lay on the clay floor of the tunnel where he had dropped it in his flight, its chimney shattered by the bullet that the man had fired at the boys. A dark puddle of oil surrounded the lantern.

Nathan picked the lantern up and shook it. "It's almost half-full!" he exclaimed. "That will give us another hour or so of light in Seth's lantern!"

The boys retraced their steps and found the side tunnel. As they started down it, Jed stopped and picked up a strange tool. It was a slender iron rod about three feet long, with a handle at one end and a claw-like projection at the other. "What is that?" Nathan asked.

"I don't know, but I can use it to mark our trail," Jed replied. As they walked along, he pressed the end of the tool into the floor every few steps, leaving a very visible trail in the dirt. He was careful to keep the claw pointed in the same direction each time, so there would be no doubt as to which direction they had come.

The tunnel opened into a maze of other tunnels. The boys tried to stay with the central one. Jed was particularly careful to make deep marks whenever there was an intersection of the corridors.

The boys had walked for about half an hour when suddenly Seth stopped. "Sh-h-h!" he whispered. "Listen!"

The boys paused, listening, hearts pounding madly. The noise grew louder. Someone was coming!

"Should we holler for help, or should we try to hide?" Seth asked of no one in particular. "It might be a friend of the man in the red shirt!"

"Let's call out for help," Jed answered. "At least, it will give us a chance!"

The boys shouted as loud as they could, their voices echoing and re-echoing in the narrow confines of the tunnel. They stopped and listened, and then yelled again.

Suddenly, Jed gave a startled gasp as a figure sprang at him from the dark shadows. The assailant knocked him to the ground. The boy threw up his hands to protect himself, then dropped them again, stunned. His assailant was . . . Wolf!

The three startled boys uttered cries of amazement, then piled on the big dog, laughing and crying at the same time. "Wolf!" Jed stammered, hugging the squirming gray animal.

"How did you get in here?"

The same thought occurred to all three boys at the same instant. If Wolf could find his way into the mine, perhaps he could lead them back out! Shouts of laughter expressed their relief at such a thought. Perhaps there was hope for them, after all!

"How did he get in here?" Nathan asked. "Why would he even want to come into a cold, dark hole like this mine?"

"This must be the way that the man in the red shirt came in," Jed suggested. "Wolf must have trailed him in here!" He looked hopefully at the dog. "Let's see if he can get us back out!"

"But it would have been so dark!" Nathan argued. "How would he find his way around in here?"

"Dogs depend on their sense of smell far more than their sense of sight," Jed replied. "If this is the route that our attacker came in, Wolf could follow his trail easily, even in the dark!"

He stood over Wolf and pointed in the direction from which the dog had come. "Go back, Wolf!" he urged. "We'll follow you!"

But the big dog didn't seem to understand, even when Jed repeated the command. He just ran around in tight circles and leaped at Jed's face, overjoyed at being reunited with his master.

"You've got to make him understand, Jed!" Nathan said. "He's our only chance! We'll never make it out of here before the light runs out, unless he shows us how he got in!"

Jed nodded soberly and tried again. "Show us the way out, Wolf!" he pleaded. "Take us back out!" But the dog still didn't understand.

"Go, Wolf, go!" Jed was desperate. He pointed down the

tunnel. "Go, Wolf!" The big dog turned and dashed down the corridor, then came tearing back toward them.

"He thinks you're playing with him!" Seth said. "He just doesn't understand."

"He's got to understand!" Jed cried out. "He's got to!" Suddenly he pulled off his belt and knelt beside the huge dog, looping the leather strap through Wolf's collar. "Home, Wolf!" he called hopefully. "Let's go home!"

The dog turned and headed back down the tunnel in the direction from which he had come. Seth and Nathan hurried to keep up. "Slow him down, Jed!" Seth called. "You'll lose us!"

Jed laughed happily. "He's got the idea now, doesn't he?" he replied.

Jed held the makeshift leash in one hand and carried his marking tool in the other. Wolf was leading him almost at a dead run, but he did his best to leave a trail with the sharp instrument, just in case they were not on the right path. Seth ran alongside them, trying desperately to keep up and light the tunnel ahead of them at the same time. Nathan held onto the tail of Seth's shirt.

"Why are we going so fast?" Nathan called out. "I can hardly keep up!"

"I'm afraid to slow Wolf down and discourage him," Jed answered over his shoulder. "Try not to step on the marks I'm making. You know, just in case!"

A few minutes later, Jed pulled back on the leash and dragged Wolf to a stop. "Look!" he cried joyfully.

It was the most beautiful sight the boys had ever seen. Up ahead, shining against the darkness of the mine tunnel, was a tiny dot of light, brilliant white in color. Daylight!

All three gave a whoop of joy, then dashed for the speck

of light. They stumbled and tripped over each other in their haste, but they all reached the opening at the same time. As badly as he wanted out, Jed held Wolf back while Nathan and Seth crawled through the opening. Jed slipped his belt from the dog's collar, then followed him through the hole.

Jed jumped to his feet as soon as he was free of the cave. It was a delight to be outside, to be free! He took a deep breath, then expelled it slowly. The prospect of a slow, terrifying death in the darkness no longer threatened them. Seth and Nathan were hugging each other when Jed crawled out, and he joined them, laughing and pounding them on the back.

"Look at you two!" Seth howled with laughter. "You're covered from head to foot with dust and grime!"

"Well, you aren't exactly Sunday-go-to-meeting clean yourself!" Nathan shouted joyfully.

The boys looked around in surprise. They had not come out in the canyon as they had expected. The terrain was strange and unfamiliar. "I think we're on the backside of Dead Man's Canyon," Jed ventured. "If we head over that hill, I think we'll come out in the canyon."

The boys hiked up the hill in the direction that Jed had pointed. They had gone fifty or sixty yards when Seth suddenly stopped. "Wait here!" he called. "I'll be right back!"

While Jed and Nathan watched, the boy ran back to the bottom of the hill. He pulled out a large, red bandana and tied it to a yucca plant near the exit of the mine. "We'll never find it again, otherwise," he explained when he rejoined the others. "That hole is pretty small!

"Well, we found the mine, but what good did it do us?" Seth remarked glumly. "The sack of gold is buried in that cave-in! No one can ever get it out now!"

Jed laughed as he patted a bulging pocket. "Did you forget what you have in your pocket?" he asked gleefully.

The boys found their horses waiting patiently where they had left them. Jed opened his saddlebag and began to stuff it with the gold nuggets from his pockets. Nathan and Seth unloaded their pockets as well, handing the heavy chunks of shiny metal to Jed.

"I didn't realize we had brought this much!" Jed said, when the last of the nuggets was safely in the leather pouch. He hefted the saddlebag. "This thing must weigh fifteen pounds!"

The boys swung gratefully into the saddles and headed for home, with Wolf trotting alongside. "Let's head for the Double-L and drop off the gold," Jed suggested. "That's probably safer than taking it into town! I wish Pa was here!"

When the boys rode into the lane at the entrance to the ranch, Mr. Laramy was mending a fence. He met them at the gate. "Yore Pa's back!" he called to Jed and Nathan. Then, he stared at their grimy faces and clothing. "Where have you lads been?"

The boys hurried into the house to find their Pa. Mr. Cartwright listened in astonishment as they told of their adventure. When they had finished, he laughed.

"Are you sure you didn't make all this up?" he asked. "This tale sounds pretty far-fetched to me!"

"Here!" Jed said as he threw the saddlebag to his Pa. "Here's proof! We brought back souvenirs of our adventure!"

The weight of the leather bag caught the big man by surprise, and it slipped through his fingers and fell to the floor with a dull thud. Mr. Cartwright picked the bag up and emptied it on the dining room table. He whistled in astonishment when he saw the contents. "Where in the world did you find all this?" he asked, as he stared at the glittering pile on the linen tablecloth. "You must have two thousand dollars here!"

The boys looked at each other happily. "Do you think it's that much?" Jed asked.

Pa nodded. "Pretty close to it, anyhow!"

He took his watch from his pocket and glanced at it. "The bank closed over two hours ago," he said. "We'll ride into town and see if Mr. Abernathy will open the vault for us. I don't think we'd better leave this here!"

Thirty minutes later, Mr. Abernathy closed the heavy vault door and spun the dial. He handed a receipt to Pa. "One hundred and forty-two troy ounces!" he said. "That's about ten pounds of pure gold!"

He smiled at the boys. "If you're splitting this three ways, that's over nine hundred dollars apiece!" The old man looked over his spectacles at Seth. "Tell your Pa to come see me in the morning," he said. "I have a feeling I'll be tearing up a mortgage!"

Mr. and Mrs. Olson stood on their front porch and listened to the whole story in astonishment. When Seth had told the part about the gold, they hugged each other for joy. "We're gonna keep the house, after all!" Mrs. Olson said happily.

"And your shop!" Jed blurted.

Mr. Olson hugged his son. "Just wait till Lou comes back!" he said, with a gleam in his eye. "She's told us again and again that Seth was good for nothing! Wait till she hears this!"

Early the next morning, Mr. Cartwright, Mr. Olson, a deputy sheriff, and several other men rode out to Dead Man's Canyon with the three boys. "Are you sure you can find the entrance again?" Mr. Olson questioned the boys.

All three nodded confidently. "Seth tied his bandana at the opening!" Nathan said. "It shouldn't be hard to find."

The party tied their horses at the entrance to the canyon, then followed the boys over the hill. The red handkerchief was easy to spot. Lanterns were lit, and one by one, the men slipped through the narrow opening in the side of the hill.

When Seth's turn came, he drew back fearfully. "It's all right, son!" the deputy said. "You don't have to go back in. One of us will stay out here with you."

But the boy stubbornly shook his head. "I'm fine," he insisted. Determined not to be left out, he took a deep breath and crawled in quickly.

Mr. Cartwright almost got stuck in the hole. He put his hands over his head and pushed and shoved his way through. His broad shoulders were almost too broad.

"Cartwright," the deputy joked, "be sure that you don't eat anything while we're in here! You'll never make it back out!"

The boys led the way through the tunnel, following Jed's trail in the clay floor. It was amazing how reassuring it was to have a dozen lanterns and a group of men along. Half an hour later, they reached the main passageway of the old Bluebird Mine and began to follow it. In moments, the group was standing at the edge of the cave-in, staring at the boot protruding from the pile of boulders.

"Poor beggar!" the deputy said. "He never had a prayer!"

"He shot at my son and his friends!" Mr. Olson blurted angrily, and the deputy took a step backwards.

"Don't get me wrong, Mr. Olson!" the deputy said. "I wasn't expressing sympathy for the fellar. He got what he deserved! But, what a way to go!"

The boys stood back a good distance as the men cautiously dug at the pile of rocks. Some of the men found extra timbers and shored up the roof for added security. It took nearly an hour, but finally the body was uncovered. The man's rifle was still in his hands, buried beneath him.

The dead man was lying face down, and the men gently rolled him over on his back. The deputy lifted the crumpled hat from the man's face, and a murmur of disbelief rippled through the little group.

Mr. Olson dropped his lantern in shock, and the sound of breaking glass reverberated throughout the quiet tunnel. "L-Lou Olson!" he stammered. "How could you?"

Encounter in the Forest

The stagecoach bounced and swayed over the rough road. Mr. Phelps was asleep, and Mr. Cartwright was busily working on some papers. Nathan sat and looked out the windows at the changing landscape. Jed held up the carving he'd finished at their last stop. "What do you think?" he whispered to Nathan. "It's for Mr. Phelps."

Nathan laughed as he examined the little figure of an owl with a schoolbook tucked under one wing. "It's great!" he decided. "Mr. Phelps will love it!"

Jed reached down and petted Wolf. "I'll be glad when we get home," he said. "I miss Ma and Ruth and Sarah!"

Nathan nodded. "I know what you mean," he said. "This trip was exciting, but I'm glad it's almost over!" He handed the woodcarving back to his brother.

"Did you see Pastor Wood's face when we gave him the money for the new church building?" Jed laughed. "I thought he was going to drop his teeth!"

"He was delighted, though, that's for sure!" Nathan added. "And I think he's right. I think more of the townspeople will come and hear the Gospel, once they have the new building up."

The boys rode in silence for a few minutes. "I'm sure gonna miss Seth," Jed said finally.

Nathan nodded. "Me too!" he agreed. "But I'm glad that the mortgage was paid off, and his family can keep their home. And wasn't that a beautiful mare that he got? He's really gonna enjoy that horse!"

The discussion turned to the subject of Seth's Aunt Lou. "I still can't believe that she would really shoot at us!" Nathan exclaimed. "I mean, she knew us, and yet she tried to kill us! And Seth was her own nephew! Why in the world would she do such a thing?"

Jed shook his head. "I haven't been able to figure that one out, either."

Mr. Cartwright set his papers aside and entered the conversation. "Greed does strange things to people!" he said. "When Seth's Aunt Lou overheard you boys talking about the mine, she wanted that gold so badly that she was willing to kill for it! And look where it got her! Remember what we were talking about on the trip out here? Money can never make anyone happy, but the lust for money can often bring misery and sorrow."

He looked at his sons. "I'm glad that you boys wanted to give the money to Pastor Wood's church. The Bible says that you will have rewards waiting for you in heaven."

"We didn't give all the money," Jed said. "Nathan and I each kept two hundred dollars!"

Pa nodded. "I know. But that was only because Pastor Wood insisted." He picked up his papers. "Oh, and one more thing," he added. "I'll replace your rifles as soon as we get home. Every boy ought to have a good rifle!"

The days turned into weeks, and the miles seemed to drag

by. The Cartwrights were anxious to get home. Finally, after many hard days of traveling, the coach arrived in St. Louis, then headed out to Meadow Green. The boys hung their heads out the windows, eager for the first glimpse of home.

The coach pulled into the Cartwright driveway, and Jed and Nathan were out the door even before it stopped. They raced for the front door of the big mansion. Mrs. Cartwright and Ruth met them at the door with hugs. "It's sure good to have you all back, safe and sound," Ma said repeatedly.

That evening at dinner, Mr. Cartwright turned to his wife. "How's the situation with the Watkins family?" he asked.

Mrs. Cartwright sighed and put down her fork. "It's certainly not improved any since you've been gone. In fact, Merle has been so unkind to Ruth that I've had Silas walk her to and from school each day."

She looked up at her big husband. "Oh, Jake, what are we going to do? Those people can be so downright cruel and unreasonable!"

The next day, Nathan and Jed went to Mississippi Valley School for the first time in several weeks. At recess, all the other students thronged the boys, eager to hear all about their adventures. The young people oohed and aahed when Jed told the story of the Bluebird Gold Mine.

Merle Watkins was the only one in the whole school who seemed uninterested in the stories that the boys had to tell. He stood aloof in the schoolyard, a scornful look on his mean face. During the next few days, he proved to be as unfriendly as ever, so the three Cartwrights simply tried to stay out of his way.

Friday afternoon, as the young people walked home from school, Mr. Cartwright came along in the surrey and gave them a ride home. "Oh, by the way, boys," he said, "Your new rifles are under the seat. I just got them today."

Jed tore open his box and looked at the new gun. It was a Spencer repeating rifle, identical to the ones that he and Nathan had left in the gold mine.

"Thanks, Pa!" the boys said in unison.

That evening, Jed stepped out the back door of the mansion with the new rifle in his hands. "Come on, boy!" he called to Wolf. "Let's go see if the squirrels are fast enough to dodge the bullets from this new gun!" Wolf bounded over to the boy, eager for a romp in the forest.

They walked through the fields and entered the woods. Jed walked along the creek bank, silently gazing at the now dry creek bed. Where the once beautiful, crystal-clear stream used to gurgle and splash over mossy rocks as it flowed merrily along, now there was nothing except an empty, silent, rocky gully. The delightful stream was now dead, thanks to Mr. Watkins and his dam. Jed sighed deeply. The creek had been his favorite spot on the entire estate, and now it was destroyed.

He and Wolf came to the split rail fence dividing Meadow Green from the Watkins property. "Better stay on this side of the fence, Wolf," he said to the big dog. "We crossed it once, but we won't make that mistake again."

Jed paused and loaded the rifle, then began to follow the fence through the woods. He shuffled through the dead, brown leaves on the ground, enjoying the rustling and crunching sound they made as he walked. Fall was his favorite time of year.

He paused, thinking he had heard a voice. He listened intently but heard nothing, so he resumed walking. Wolf began digging for a mouse hiding in the leaves.

Jed stopped. There it was again! He was sure of it this

time. Someone was calling for help! "Come on, Wolf!" Jed called to the big dog. "It sounds like someone needs our help! Let's go see!"

The voice called again, and this time, there was no longer any doubt in Jed's mind. Someone was in trouble! The boy and the dog began to run in the direction of the cry, and suddenly Jed hesitated. They had come to Mr. Watkins' fence, and he wasn't about to cross that!

But the urgency in the voice that Jed had heard made him reconsider. From the sound of things, someone was in desperate trouble! Taking a deep breath, the boy climbed up on the fence. "Hurry, Wolf," he said, "under the fence!"

Wolf scrambled under the fence and Jed quickly jumped down. The boy and the dog dashed through the woods. And then they came upon a scene that sent a cold chill up and down Jed's spine.

Mr. Watkins, the neighbor that had caused so much trouble for the Cartwrights, was lying on the ground with his back against a fallen log. His leg was caught in the steel jaws of a large trap! Three or four feet away, just beyond the reach of his outstretched fingers, lay the man's shotgun. And creeping toward the desperate man was a large, gray wolf!

The Wolf

Jed took in the situation at a glance. Mr. Watkins could not reach his weapon. The wolf, unaware of the presence of the boy or the dog, was directly between them and the injured man. Jed did not dare risk a shot at the wolf from where he stood.

The fallen man looked up, a pleading expression on his drawn face. His belligerence and unfriendliness were gone. "You've got to help me, boy!" the man pleaded. "You've got to! This animal has the staggers! Iffen he bites me, I'm done for!" He stretched out his hand toward the boy as the wolf crept closer. "Please, boy, I'm begging you! Let bygones be bygones! You've got to help me!"

Jed dashed to one side, hoping to get a better angle for a shot at the rabid wolf. The snarling animal was now only two or three steps from the cringing man. His fangs were bared, and foamy saliva dripped from his jaws. Jed quickly cocked the rifle, realizing that he was only going to get one shot in. That one shot would have to count.

But as Jed found the wolf in his rifle sights, a gray streak of fur suddenly struck the wolf, bowling him over. Jed's brave dog was in the battle! Growling and snapping, the huge dog leaped at the wolf a second time.

But the wolf was ready. His crazed mind had already forgotten the man on the ground, and now his attention was on this impertinent dog that had dared to attack him. As Wolf sprang, the wild animal leaped nimbly to one side, slashing with his fangs at the dog.

Holding the rifle ready, Jed ran in closer, hoping for a clear shot. "Careful, boy!" Mr. Watkins called. "That wolf has hydrophoby! Iffen he bites you, yo're done for!"

The wolf and the dog rolled over and over, snarling, snapping, and slashing. The boy leaped back suddenly as the fighting animals nearly landed on top of him. He held his fire, afraid of hitting his dog if he shot at the wolf.

But suddenly, the vicious wolf sprang clear of the dog just for an instant, and Jed saw his chance. He fired, and knew immediately that he had hit the wolf. But the shot had no effect whatever. Blood poured from his side, but the big animal continued to fight as though he had not even been hit. He sprang at the dog again, growling furiously.

Jed levered another shell into the chamber of the rifle. He raised the gun, hoping for another clear shot. "Shoot, boy, shoot!" the man on the ground cried, but Jed still hesitated. He would not fire and take a chance on hitting his beloved dog!

The wolf slashed at Wolf's flank, and the big dog let out a yelp of pain. Something snapped inside Jed when he heard Wolf's cry, and he forgot all about the danger involved. He ran in close to the fighting animals. He had to kill that wolf!

The wolf raised his head for an instant, and Jed knew it was now or never. He pulled the trigger, and the gun roared a second time. The wolf leaped into the air, rolled over, then came straight at Jed!

But the boy had already cocked the rifle again, and as the animal leaped, he fired. To his immense relief, the wolf fell to the ground. Jed stepped closer and fired once more, just to be sure. The wolf lay still. He was finally dead.

"You took an awful chance, boy!" Mr. Watkins called from the ground. "I'm sure that wolf had hydrophoby!"

Jed nodded. "But I couldn't let him kill you or my dog!"

He glanced over at Wolf. The big dog was licking some bloody wounds, but he seemed to be all right. Jed breathed a sigh of relief.

He knelt beside the man and looked at the trap. Strong steel jaws had snapped their jagged teeth closed on Mr. Watkins' leg. The man's trouser leg was torn and bloody, and the steel teeth were imbedded deeply. Jed winced as he looked at the injury.

"I jumped over this log when the wolf came at me the first time," the man explained through clenched teeth. "I landed right in this bear trap, and I dropped my shotgun when it got me. If you hadn't come along, that wolf would have got me for sure!"

Suddenly, the man seemed embarrassed. "Son," he said softly, "Merle and I have got a lot of making up to do! My boy and I have treated you folks like trash, and I'm genuinely sorry. I'm really not sure why you even helped me today!"

The injured man looked up at Jed, almost as if he was afraid. "Can you forgive us, Son?" he pleaded. "I don't know how, but somehow we'll make it up to you!"

Jed's heart softened as he heard the man's repentant words. Suddenly, all the hatred and resentment that he had felt toward this obnoxious man were gone. He smiled. "That's all right, Mr. Watkins," he said softly. "And if I know Pa, he's willing to forgive you, too!"

The man on the ground looked relieved. "You're good people," he said. "I am really sorry for all the trouble we caused." He looked up at Jed again. "I'll have my men tear out the dam first thing tomorrow! It'll take a little while, but your creek will soon be back to normal. Even the fish and crawdads will come back, I promise."

He suddenly winced in pain, and his attention was drawn back to the trap. "Can you help me get this wretched trap off my leg? It's about to cut my foot off!" He gritted his teeth, then turned back to Jed. "See if you can find two short logs. One of them should be about this thick." He held his hands up, about five or six inches apart. "I'll show you how to spring the trap."

Jed hurried through the woods, and returned in a moment with two fallen branches. "This is all I could find right away."

The man nodded, then winced again. "That's good," he groaned. "They'll do fine." He took one of the branches from the boy. "Here," he said, pointing. "Push down on this lever as hard as you can with that branch. That will take some of the tension off the trap spring. I'll see if I can slip this branch in between the end of the jaws, and hold them open long enough to get my leg out." He looked at Jed. "Understand?"

Jed nodded.

"Good! Ready? Here goes!"

Jed leaned on the branch with all his might, pushing with his full weight on the lever of the trap. The jaws opened slightly. "Just a little more!" Mr. Watkins called weakly.

Jed went at it again, and the trap opened just a little wider. "Good! Hold it right there for just a second!" the man begged as he inserted the branch at the end of the steel jaws. Gritting his teeth, he reached down and squeezed his leg, pulling the flesh free from the sharp steel teeth. He carefully lifted his foot, and his leg was free! When he bumped the branch slightly, the wicked steel jaws slammed shut with a snap that made Jed flinch.

The man laughed weakly. "These things are nasty, aren't they?" he said.

As Jed watched, the neighbor leaned back against the log and tore a strip of cloth from his shirt. He wrapped the makeshift bandage tightly around the injured leg. "I'm bleedin' pretty badly," he told the boy. "Can you help me to the house?"

Jed stood up. "Why don't I run to your place and get a horse and some help?" he suggested. "The way you're bleeding, I'm afraid you can't walk!"

The man shook his head. "One of my men might shoot you," he said. "I'd be afraid to have you go up there alone!"

"Then I'll go to my house," Jed said. "I'll be back in just a couple minutes with some help and a horse." He turned away, but the man called him back.

"Jed?"

"Yes, sir?"

"Thanks for helping me, Son. I know I didn't deserve it!" He looked sadly at the boy. "I'm awful sorry about yore dog!"

Jed glanced over to where Wolf lay in the grass, licking his wounds. "He's all right, Mr. Watkins," he said. "He got cut up some, but he'll be all right! He's one tough dog!"

The man slowly shook his head. "You don't understand, Son! He won't be all right! That wolf had hydrophoby! And yore dog got bit several times!"

Jed stared at the man. "You mean he might get—"

Mr. Watkins nodded. "I'm afraid so, Jed! Yore dog will have to be destroyed!" He buried his face in his hands. "And it's all on account of me! I'm sorry, lad, very, very sorry!"

"He'll be all right!" Jed said curtly, afraid to believe the truth. "He didn't get bitten that bad. He's gonna be all right!"

But the injured neighbor just shook his head. "I'm sorry, Son. How I wish that were true! But, you don't git bit by a mad wolf and walk away from it. I'm sorry, boy, but yore dog doesn't have a chance!"

The Verdict

Jed turned and ran blindly through the woods. Tears stung his eyes. Wolf wouldn't die! He couldn't! Mr. Watkins was wrong!

In spite of his wounds, the big dog jumped to his feet and ran after his young master. The boy ran blindly into a low hanging branch and was knocked to the ground. Wolf jumped on him, licking his face.

Jed hugged the giant dog briefly, then remembered the urgency of getting help for Mr. Watkins. He sprang to his feet. "You'll be all right, Wolf!" he called to the dog. "I promise you!"

Jed found Pa in the barn and quickly blurted out the story of the rabid wolf's attack. The big man dropped the pitchfork he was working with. "Tell Nathan to ride for Doc Barker!" he called to Silas, who was pitching hay. "Have him come to the Watkins' house!"

He hurried from the barn. "It'll take too long to try to get a horse across that fence and through the woods," he told Jed. "We'll just carry Mr. Watkins ourselves!" He ran across the field toward the woods.

Jed made Wolf lie down beside the barn, then raced after his father, trying to match the tall man's giant strides. He finally caught up when his father reached the fence.

"This way!" he called, then dashed through the woods with Pa on his heels. Mr. Watkins lay where Jed had left him, his face pale from the loss of blood. The leg wound was still bleeding. Mr. Cartwright knelt beside him.

The neighbor weakly held up one hand. "Jake," he whispered, "I'm sorry for all the harm we done to you and yore family. Yore boy here saved my life! I owe you, Jake! And I aim to make it up to you!"

But Pa just shook his head and took the man's hand. "If you're willing, neighbor," he said, "both of us will just start with a clean slate, starting today! It's time for us to get busy being good neighbors."

He took a quick look at the man's leg, then tore a wide section out of his own shirt. He pulled the bandage tight around the injured leg to stop the flow of blood. "We've gotta get you to the house," he said. "Doc Barker should be on his way to have a look at you." He stooped over and picked up the man, cradling him in his arms. Jed marveled again at the tremendous strength of his Pa, and the ease with which he carried Mr. Watkins.

When they reached the neighbor's house, one of Mr. Watkins' hired men met them at the back door. "What's goin' on?" he snarled at Mr. Cartwright.

Mr. Watkins spoke sharply. "Paul! These people are our neighbors! I owe my life to them today! We all owe them an apology."

The man looked confused but held the door open for Mr. Cartwright. As he was carried through the door, Mr. Watkins turned and addressed the man again. "Paul!"

"Yes, sir."

"Get the men, and tear out the dam we built in the woods. I want the creek restored to the way it was before we started messing with it! If possible, I want it finished by tomorrow night!"

The man looked surprised. "Yes, sir!" he answered as he turned away.

Doc Barker arrived a few minutes later and began to work with his patient. Pa leaned over and spoke to Mr. Watkins. "Is there anything we can do to help before we leave?"

The man slowly shook his head. "Neighbor," he said, "you and yore boy have done enough. You saved my life!" He turned to Jed. "Thanks, Son."

As they walked home, Jed haltingly told Pa what Mr. Watkins had said about Wolf. "It isn't true, is it, Pa?" Jed pleaded. "Wolf could be all right, couldn't he? Just because he was bitten by the wolf doesn't mean that he has to catch the hydrophobia, does it?"

The big man turned and regarded his son with a sorrowful expression. "Usually it does, Jed. I've seen animals get the disease and go stark raving mad, staggering around like they were drunk, biting at everything in sight! We don't want that to happen to Wolf, do we? When an animal with hydrophobia bites a dog, the best thing to do is to destroy the dog. I know that's hard, Son, but that's the only way."

Jed suddenly burst into tears. "But, we can't kill Wolf! We just can't!" He looked up at his huge father, his eyes pleading. "Please, Pa! Tell me that Wolf will be all right!"

Mr. Cartwright's heart went out to his son. He knew only too well what the huge gray dog meant to the boy. How could he tell Jed that his beloved dog had to be destroyed? He put a big arm around the heart-broken boy. "Let's ask Doc

Barker," he suggested gently. "If Wolf has any chance at all, Doc Barker will tell us." The big man brushed a tear out of his own eye, then continued. "We'll go see the doc right after supper."

Jed found he couldn't eat a bit of supper. While the rest of the family ate, he went out to the barn and washed the big dog's wounds. They didn't look that bad! Why couldn't Wolf be all right? Maybe Pa and Mr. Watkins were wrong!

When Mr. Cartwright came out to the barn to saddle two horses for the trip to Doc Barker's, Jed was leaning dejectedly against the barn. The man walked up and stood beside his son. He cleared his throat, then spoke in a voice that was strangely husky. "Jed," he said, "I just want you to know that I care about Wolf, too. Whatever happens, Son, I want you to know I really care."

The boy looked up and nodded. "Thanks, Pa." They saddled the horses and rode to the doctor's house. Fear tightened Jed's stomach in knots as they approached the house. "Please, God," he pleaded silently, "let Wolf be all right! Please, God!"

Doc Barker had only been home a few minutes, but he welcomed the two visitors warmly. "Come in, Jake. Well, hello, Jed. What's on your minds?"

The two Cartwrights went into the house and Jed stepped forward. "Doc," he said, "my dog was bitten by the wolf several times this afternoon! Mr. Watkins says that the wolf had hydrophobia, and that my dog will catch it, too! Is that true?"

The doctor became very sober. "Sit down, Jed," he said. The boy sat down on the sofa and the doctor sat beside him. "I'm afraid there have been some cases of hydrophobia in this area lately. And from what Mr. Watkins told me about the way the wolf was acting, it sounds like the wolf had it."

He paused, weighing his words carefully. "Jed," he said, "if your dog was bitten by a rabid wolf, he's almost certain to catch the disease. I know this is hard for you, and it's hard for me to say it, but it would be better for your dog if we shot him now, instead of waiting for him to develop hydrophobia."

The man laid a hand on Jed's shoulder. "I'm sorry, Son. I wish there was something I could do."

"But Wolf may not catch it!" Jed protested. "Couldn't we just wait and see?" Tears welled up in his eyes as he continued, "Maybe the wolf didn't have it! Maybe he—" A sob choked off his words.

Doc Barker shook his head. "Hydrophobia is a dreadful thing, Son. When I was younger I knew a man that was bitten by a rabid coon. When he realized that he was going to get the disease, he chained himself to a tree so he wouldn't be able to attack his wife and children. When the disease struck, he went completely crazy. He died a horrible death. You don't take chances with hydrophobia!"

Jed was desperate. "Couldn't we chain Wolf somewhere," he begged, "and just watch him to see if he has it? If he has it, then I guess you'll have to . . ." The boy's voice trailed off.

Doc Barker looked up at Pa and shrugged. Both men knew the situation was hopeless.

"How long does it take the disease to develop?" Pa asked.

"Two to four weeks, normally," the physician replied. "The symptoms show up pretty fast."

"What if we were to lock Wolf up for four weeks?" Pa suggested. "You could observe him at the end of that time, and if you think he has the hydrophobia, well, then I guess I'd have to shoot him."

The doctor looked thoughtful. "You'd be taking an awful chance, Jake!" he said hesitantly. "If the dog were to get loose and bite one of you, well . . ."

"We'll lock him in the corncrib!" Mr. Cartwright declared. "And I'll chain him, too. Then we'll know for sure that he can't get loose."

Doc Barker nodded. "I guess that would be fairly safe," he agreed. "But let me caution you, Jake. Don't let anyone near that corncrib, not even Jed! When you feed Wolf, make dead sure you stay clear of him, even if his behavior seems normal!"

Pa nodded. "We won't take any chances!"

As Jed and Pa left the doctor's house, the man put a hand on Jed's shoulder. "Son," he said gently, "don't get your hopes too high. There's not one chance in a thousand that Wolf is going to escape the hydrophobia. I hope for your sake that he does, but his chances aren't very good. Understand?"

Jed nodded and followed his pa outside. They rode home in silence. Pa went out and secured Wolf in the corncrib. Jed couldn't bring himself to even watch.

The next few days were torture for the boy. He couldn't sleep at night, he had completely lost his appetite, and he began to do poorly at school. All through the day he prayed that God would spare his dog from getting hydrophobia.

There was one bright spot during those trying days. On Monday, Merle caught up with the Cartwrights as they walked to school. He hesitantly approached Jed and extended his hand. "I'm sorry, Jed," he said meekly, "for everything! Thank you for what you did for my Pa." He looked Jed in the eye. "I hope Wolf makes it. I really do!"

Jed nodded and shook the boy's hand. "Thank you, Merle," he said quietly.

Early one morning, Jed was awakened by the sound of the back door slamming. He jumped from his bed and rushed to the window, brushing the curtain to one side. Pa was walking across the yard. He had already passed the reflection garden and had almost reached the barn. In one hand he carried a rifle.

In an instant, Jed realized what Pa was going to do. He was heading for the corncrib! "No, Pa, no!" he screamed as he dashed from the room. The panic-stricken boy dashed down the stairs in his pajamas. As he threw open the back door, a shot rang out, and then another.

Jed's heart seemed to stop at the sound of the gunshots. It was too late to save his beloved Wolf! Bare feet flying, Jed dashed around the corner of the barn by the corncrib to confront his father.

"How could you, Pa!" he screamed. "How could you? You know what Wolf means to me! How could you shoot my dog?"

Mr. Cartwright turned and faced the boy, a surprised look on his face. The rifle was still in his hands.

Jed ran up to his father and seized the rifle. "How could you, Pa?" he cried again. Then he stopped and stared at the ground behind his Pa. The body of a dead coon lay in the grass at the edge of the cornfield. Jed spun around and ran to the corncrib. Wolf leaped to greet him with a joyful bark. Jed just stared at the dog, then turned back to his father.

"I'm sorry, Pa," he said. "When I heard the gun, I thought you had . . ."

Pa came over and put his arm around Jed. "I know, Son," he said quietly. "I've been praying every day that we wouldn't have to shoot your dog!"

He pointed at the body of the coon. "I think I finally got the varmint that's been feasting on our corn all this summer. I'm sorry that the shots scared you."

The big man pulled his watch from his pocket and glanced at it. "Better get ready for school, Son." He handed the rifle to Jed. "The four weeks are almost up. I'm gonna go see if Doc will come and take a look at Wolf today. I've been watching him myself, and frankly, I don't see anything wrong with him. I think he's gonna be all right! But we need to wait and see what Doc Barker says."

When Jed walked out of school that afternoon, Wolf was waiting at the fence for him. Beside the big dog stood Pa, a huge grin on his face. Jed took one look at the pair and then gave a joyful whoop as he dashed across the schoolyard. Wolf was going to be all right!

After supper that evening, Jed and Wolf walked across the fields. The boy laughed as the dog chased a groundhog into his hole. When they reached the creek, Jed sat on the bank and leaned back against an elm. He watched the water flowing merrily along, splashing and laughing on its journey. The creek was back!

A lone minnow darted across a deep pool. Jed scanned the water carefully but could see no others. "There'll be others soon," he told Wolf. "They'll swim downstream like this little fellar did and decide to just stay and live here. Before long, the fish and crawdads will be back, too. Our creek is coming back! God sure has been good to us, hasn't He?"

The big dog just wagged his tail. Jed put an arm around Wolf, and the two of them watched the sunset reflected in the waters of the little creek.

About the Author

Ed Dunlop has worked with children and young people as an evangelist since 1975. He and his family travel most of the year conducting Kids' Crusades. When not traveling, the Dunlop family resides in north Georgia.